CHALIAPINE AS CZAR BORIS.

HENRY EDWARD KREHBIEL

A SECOND
BOOK OF OPERAS

GARDEN CITY, NEW YORK
GARDEN CITY PUBLISHING CO., INC.

TO

RICHARD ALDRICH

OLD AND FAITHFUL FRIEND, GRACIOUS COLLEAGUE,
KIND HELPER

„Freundschaft ist ein Knotenstock auf Reisen.“
— Chamisso.

CONTENTS AND INDEX

CHAPTER I

BIBLICAL OPERAS

CHAPTER II

BIBLE STORIES IN OPERA AND ORATORIO

CHAPTER III

RUBINSTEIN AND HIS "GEISTLICHE OPER"

CHAPTER IV

"SAMSON ET DALILA"

CHAPTER V

"DIE KÖNIGIN VON SABA"

CHAPTER IX

"CAVALLERIA RUSTICANA"

CHAPTER X

THE CAREER OF MASCAGNI

CHAPTER XI

" IRIS "

CHAPTER XIV

"KÖNIGSKINDER"

CHAPTER XV

"BORIS GODOUNOFF"

CHAPTER XVI

"MADAME SANS-GÊNE" AND OTHER OPERAS
BY GIORDANO

CHAPTER XVII

TWO OPERAS BY WOLF-FERRARI

A SECOND BOOK OF OPERAS

CHAPTER I

BIBLICAL OPERAS

WHETHER or not the English owe a grudge to their
Lord Chamberlain for depriving them of the pleasure of seeing operas based on Biblical stories I do
not know. If they do, the grudge cannot be a deep
one, for it is a long time since Biblical operas were in
vogue, and in the case of the very few survivals it
has been easy to solve the difficulty and salve the
conscience of the public censor by the simple device of
changing the names of the characters and the scene
of action if the works are to be presented on the
stage, or omitting scenery, costumes and action and
performing them as oratorios. In either case, when-
ever this has been done, however, it has been the habit
of critics to make merry at the expense of my Lord
Chamberlain and the puritanicalness of the popular
spirit of which he is supposed to be the official embod-
iment, and to discourse lugubriously and mayhap
profoundly on the perversion of composers' purposes
and the loss of things essential to the lyric drama.

It may be heretical to say so, but is it not possible that Lord Chamberlain and Critic have both taken too serious a view of the matter? There is a vast amount of admirable material in the Bible (historical, legendary or mythical, as one happens to regard it), which would not necessarily be degraded by dramatic treatment, and which might be made entertaining as well as edifying, as it has been made in the past, by stage representation. Reverence for this material is neither inculcated nor preserved by shifting the scene and throwing a veil over names too transparent to effect a disguise. Moreover, when this is done, there is always danger that the process may involve a sacrifice of the respect to which a work of art is entitled on its merits as such. Gounod, in collaboration with Barbier and Carré, wrote an opera entitled "La Reine de Saba." The plot had nothing to do with the Bible beyond the name of Sheba's Queen and King Solomon. Mr. Farnie, who used to make comic operetta books in London, adapted the French libretto for performance in English and called the opera "Irene." What a title for a grand opera! Why not "Blanche" or "Arabella"? No doubt such a thought flitted through many a careless mind unconscious that an Irene was a Byzantine Empress of the eighth century, who, by her devotion to its tenets, won beatification after death from the Greek Church. The opera failed on the Continent as well as in London, but if it had not been given a comic operetta flavor by its title and association with the name of the excellent Mr. Farnie, would the change in supposed time, place and people have harmed it?

A few years ago I read (with amusement, of course) of the metamorphosis to which Massenet's "Hérodiade" was subjected so that it might masquerade for a brief space on the London stage; but when I saw the opera in New York "in the original package" (to speak commercially), I could well believe that the music sounded the same in London, though John the Baptist sang under an alias and the painted scenes were supposed to delineate Ethiopia instead of Palestine.

There is a good deal of nonsensical affectation in the talk about the intimate association in the minds of composers of music, text, incident, and original purpose. "Un Ballo in Maschera," as we see it most often nowadays, plays in Nomansland; but I fancy that its music would sound pretty much the same if the theatre of action were transplanted back to Sweden, whence it came originally, or left in Naples, whither it emigrated, or in Boston, to which highly inappropriate place it was banished to oblige the Neapolitan censor. So long as composers have the habit of plucking feathers out of their dead birds to make wings for their new, we are likely to remain in happy and contented ignorance of *mésalliances* between music and score, until they are pointed out by too curious critics or confessed by the author. What is present habit was former custom to which no kind or degree of stigma attached. Bach did it; Handel did it; nor was either of these worthies always scrupulous in distinguishing between *meum* and *tuum* when it came to appropriating existing thematic material. In their day the merit of individuality and the right of property lay more in the manner in which ideas were presented than in the ideas themselves.

In 1886 I spent a delightful day with Dr. Chrysander at his home in Bergedorf, near Hamburg, and he told me the story of how on one occasion, when Keiser was incapacitated by the vice to which he was habitually prone, Handel, who sat in his orchestra, was asked by him to write the necessary opera. Handel complied, and his success was too great to leave Keiser's mind in peace. So he reset the book. Before Keiser's setting was ready for production Handel had gone to Italy. Hearing of Keiser's act, he secured a copy of the new setting from a member of the orchestra and sent back to Hamburg a composition based on Keiser's melodies "to show how such themes ought to be treated." Dr. Chrysander, also, when he gave me a copy of Bertati's "Don Giovanni" libretto, for which Gazzaniga composed the music, told me that Mozart had been only a little less free than the poet in appropriating ideas from the older work.

One of the best pieces in the final scene of "Fidelio" was taken from a cantata on the death of the emperor of Austria, composed by Beethoven before he left Bonn. The melody originally conceived for the

last movement of the Symphony in D minor was
developed into the finale of one of the last string
quartets. In fact the instances in which composers
have put their pieces to widely divergent purposes
are innumerable and sometimes amusing, in view
of the fantastic belief that they are guided by
plenary inspiration. The overture which Rossini
wrote for his "Barber of Seville" was lost soon
after the first production of the opera. The composer did not take the trouble to write another,
but appropriated one which had served its purpose
in an earlier work. Persons ignorant of that fact,
but with lively imaginations, as I have said in one
of my books,[1] have rhapsodized on its appositeness,
and professed to hear in it the whispered plottings
of the lovers and the merry raillery of *Rosina* contrasted with the futile ragings of her grouty guardian ;
but when Rossini composed this piece of music its
mission was to introduce an adventure of the Emperor Aurelianus in Palmyra in the third century
of the Christian era. Having served that purpose
it became the prelude to another opera which dealt
with Queen Elizabeth of England, a monarch who
reigned some twelve hundred years after Aurelianus.
Again, before the melody now known as that of
Almaviva's cavatina had burst into the efflorescence
which now distinguishes it, it came as a chorus
from the mouths of Cyrus and his Persians in ancient
Babylon.

[1] "A Book of Operas," p. 9.

When Mr. Lumley desired to produce Verdi's "Nabucodonosor" (called "Nabucco" for short) in London in 1846 he deferred to English tradition and brought out the opera as "Nino, Rè d'Assyria." I confess that I cannot conceive how changing a king of Babylon to a king of Assyria could possibly have brought about a change one way or the other in the effectiveness of Verdi's Italian music, but Mr. Lumley professed to have found in the transformation reason for the English failure. At any rate, he commented, in his "Reminiscences of the Opera," "That the opera thus lost much of its original character, especially in the scene where the captive Israelites became very uninteresting Babylonians, and was thereby shorn of one element of success present on the Continent, is undeniable."

There is another case even more to the purpose of this present discussion. In 1818 Rossini produced his opera "Mosè in Egitto" in Naples. The strength of the work lay in its choruses; yet two of them were borrowed from the composer's "Armida." In 1822 Bochsa performed it as an oratorio at Covent Garden, but, says John Ebers in his "Seven Years of the King's Theatre," published in 1828, "the audience accustomed to the weighty metal and pearls of price of Handel's compositions found the 'Moses' as dust in the balance in comparison." "The oratorio having failed as completely as erst did Pharaoh's host," Ebers continues, "the ashes of 'Mosè in Egitto' revived in

the form of an opera entitled 'Pietro l'Eremita.'
Moses was transformed into *Peter*. In this form
the opera was as successful as it had been unfortunate as an oratorio. . . . 'Mosè in Egitto' was
condemned as cold, dull, and heavy. 'Pietro
l'Eremita,' Lord Sefton, one of the most competent judges of the day, pronounced to be the most
effective opera produced within his recollection;
and the public confirmed the justice of the remark,
for no opera during my management had such un-
equivocal success." [1] This was not the end of the
opera's vicissitudes, to some of which I shall recur
presently; let this suffice now:

Rossini rewrote it in 1827, adding some new music
for the Académie Royal in Paris, and called it
"Moïse"; when it was revived for the Covent
Garden oratorios, London, in 1833, it was not only
performed with scenery and dresses, but recruited
with music from Handel's oratorio and renamed
"The Israelites in Egypt; or the Passage of the
Red Sea"; when the French "Moïse" reached
the Royal Italian Opera, Covent Garden, in April,
1850, it had still another name, "Zora," though
Chorley does not mention the fact in his "Thirty
Years' Musical Recollections," probably because
the failure of the opera which he loved grieved
him too deeply. For a long time "Moses" occupied a prominent place among oratorios. The

[1] "Seven Years of the King's Theatre," by John Ebers,
pp. 157, 158.

Handel and Haydn Society of Boston adopted it in 1845, and between then and 1878 performed it forty-five times.

In all the years of my intimate association with the lyric drama (considerably more than the number of which Mr. Chorley has left us a record) I have seen but one opera in which the plot adheres to the Biblical story indicated by its title. That opera is Saint-Saëns's "Samson et Dalila." I have seen others whose titles and *dramatis personæ* suggested narratives found in Holy Writ, but in nearly all these cases it would be a profanation of the Book to call them Biblical operas. Those which come to mind are Goldmark's "Königin von Saba," Massenet's "Hérodiade" and Richard Strauss's "Salome." I have heard, in whole or part, but not seen, three of the works which Rubinstein would fain have us believe are operas, but which are not — "Das verlorene Paradies," "Der Thurmbau zu Babel" and "Moses"; and I have a study acquaintance with the books and scores of his "Maccabäer," which is an opera; his "Sulamith," which tries to be one, and his "Christus," which marks the culmination of the vainest effort that a contemporary composer made to parallel Wagner's achievement on a different line. There are other works which are sufficiently known to me through library communion or concert-room contact to enable me to claim enough acquaintanceship to justify converse about them and which must perforce occupy attention in this study. Chiefest and noblest of these are Rossini's "Moses" and Méhul's "Joseph." Finally, there are a few with which I have only a passing or speaking acquaintance; whose faces I can recognize, fragments of whose speech I know, and whose repute is such that I can contrive to guess at their hearts — such as Verdi's "Nabucodonosor" and Gounod's "Reine de Saba."

Rossini's "Moses" was the last of the Italian operas (the last by a significant composer, at least) which used to be composed to ease the Lenten conscience in pleasure-loving Italy. Though written to be played with the adjuncts of scenery and costumes, it has less of action than might easily be infused into a performance of Mendelssohn's "Elijah," and the epical element which finds its exposition in the choruses is far greater than that in any opera of its time with which I am acquainted. In both its aspects, as oratorio and as opera, it harks back to a time when the two forms were essentially the same save in respect of subject matter. It is a convenient working hypothesis to take the classic tragedy of Hellas as the progenitor of the opera. It can also be taken as the prototype of the Festival of the Ass, which was celebrated as long ago as the twelfth century in France; of the miracle plays which were performed in England at the same time; the *Commedia spirituale* of thirteenth-century Italy and the *Geistliche Schauspiele* of fourteenth-century Germany. These mummeries, with their admixture of church song, pointed the way as media of edification to the dramatic representations of Biblical scenes which Saint Philip Neri used to attract audiences to hear his sermons in the Church of St. Mary in Vallicella, in Rome, and the sacred musical dramas came to be called oratorios. While the *camerata* were seeking to revive the classic drama in Florence, Carissimi was experimenting with sacred material in Rome, and his epoch-making allegory, "La Rappresentazione dell' Anima e del Corpo," was brought out, almost simultaneously with Peri's "Euridice," in 1600. Putting off the fetters of plainsong, music became beautiful for its own sake, and as an agent of dramatic expression. His excursions into Biblical story were followed for a century or more by the authors of *sacra azione*, written to take the place of secular operas in Lent. The stories of Jephtha and his daughter, Hezekiah, Belshazzar, Abraham and Isaac, Jonah, Job, the Judgment of Solomon, and the Last Judgment became the staple of opera composers in Italy and Germany for more than a century. Alessandro Scarlatti, whose name looms large in the history of opera, also composed oratorios; and Mr. E. J. Dent, his biographer, has pointed out that "except that the operas are in three acts and the oratorios in two, the only difference is in the absence of professedly comic characters and of the formal statement in which the author protests that the words *fato, dio, dieta,* etc., are only *scherzi poetici* and imply nothing contrary to the Catholic faith." Zeno and Metastasio wrote texts for sacred operas as well as profane, with Tobias, Absalom, Joseph, David, Daniel, and Sisera as subjects.

Presently I shall attempt a discussion of the gigantic attempt made by Rubinstein to enrich the stage with an art-form to which he gave a distinctive name, but which was little else than an inflated type of the old *sacra azione,* employing the larger apparatus which modern invention and enterprise have placed at the command of the playwright, stage manager, and composer. I am compelled to see in his project chiefly a jealous ambition to rival the great and triumphant accomplishment of Richard Wagner, but it is possible that he had a prescient eye on a coming time. The desire to combine pictures with oratorio has survived the practice which prevailed down to the beginning of the nineteenth century. Handel used scenes and costumes when he produced his "Esther," as well as his "Acis and Galatea," in London. Dittersdorf has left for us a description of the stage decorations prepared for his oratorios when they were performed in the palace of the Bishop of Groswardein. Of late years there have been a number of theatrical representations of Mendelssohn's "Elijah." I have witnessed as well as heard a performance of "Acis and Galatea" and been entertained with the spectacle of *Polyphemus* crush-

ing the head of presumptuous *Acis* with a stave
like another *Fafner* while singing "Fly, thou massy
ruin, fly" to the bludgeon which was playing under-
study for the fatal rock.

This diverting incident brings me to a consideration of one of the difficulties which stand in the
way of effective stage pictures combined with
action in the case of some of the most admired
of the subjects for oratorios or sacred opera. It
was not the Lord Chamberlain who stood in the
way of Saint-Saëns's "Samson et Dalila" in the
United States for many years, but the worldly
wisdom of opera managers who shrank from attempt-
ing to stage the spectacle of the falling Temple of
Dagon, and found in the work itself a plentiful
lack of that dramatic movement which is to-day
considered more essential to success than beautiful
and inspiriting music. "Samson et Dalila" was
well known in its concert form when the management of the Metropolitan Opera House first attempted to introduce it as an opera. It had a
single performance in the season of 1894–1895 and
then sought seclusion from the stage lamps for
twenty years. It was, perhaps, fortunate for the
work that no attempt was made to repeat it, for,
though well sung and satisfactorily acted, the top-
pling of the pillars of the temple, discreetly sup-
ported by too visible wires, at the conclusion made
a stronger appeal to the popular sense of the ridic-
ulous than even Saint-Saëns's music could with-

stand. It is easy to inveigh against the notion
that frivolous fribbles and trumpery trappings
should receive more attention than the fine music
which ought to be recognized as the soul of the
work, the vital spark which irradiates an inconse-
quential material body; but human nature has
not yet freed itself sufficiently from gross clogs to
attain so ideal an attitude.

It is to a danger similar to that which threatened
the original New York "Samson" that the world
owes the most popular melody in Rossini's "Mosè."
The story is old and familiar to the students of
operatic history, but will bear retelling. The plague
of darkness opens the opera, the passage of the
Red Sea concludes it. Rossini's stage manager
had no difficulty with the former, which demanded
nothing more than the lowering of the stage lights.
But he could evolve no device which could save the
final miracle from laughter. A hilarious ending to
so solemn a work disturbed the management and
the librettist, Totola, who, just before a projected
revival in Naples, a year or two after the first
production, came to the composer with a project
for saving the third act. Rossini was in bed, as
usual, and the poet showed him the text of the
prayer, "Dal tuo stellato," which he said he had
written in an hour. "I will get up and write the
music," said Rossini; "you shall have it in a quarter
of an hour." And he kept his word, whether literally or not in respect of time does not matter. When

the opera was again performed it contained the
chorus with its melody which provided Paganini
with material for one of his sensational performances
on the G-string.

Carpani tells the story and describes the effect
upon the audience which heard it for the first time.
Laughter was just beginning in the pit when the
public was surprised to note that *Moses* was about
to sing. The people stopped laughing and prepared to listen. They were awed by the beauty
of the minor strain which was echoed by *Aaron*
and then by the chorus of *Israelites*. The host
marched across the mimic sea and fell on its knees,
and the music burst forth again, but now in the
major mode. And now the audience joined in the
jubilation. The people in the boxes, says Carpani,
stood up; they leaned over the railings; applauded;
they shouted: "Bello! bello! O che bello!" Carpani adds: "I am almost in tears when I think of
this prayer." An impressionable folk, those Italians
of less than a century ago. "Among other things
that can be said in praise of our hero," remarked a

physician to Carpani, amidst the enthusiasm caused by the revamped opera, "do not forget that he is an assassin. I can cite to you more than forty attacks of nervous fever or violent convulsions on the part of young women, fond to excess of music, which have no other origin than the prayer of the Hebrews in the third act with its superb change of key !"

Thus music saved the scene in Naples. When the opera was rewritten for London and made to tell a story about Peter the Hermit, the corresponding scene had to be elided after the first performance. Ebers tells the story: "A body of troops was supposed to pass over a bridge which, breaking, was to precipitate them into the water. The troops being made of basketwork and pulled over the bridge by ropes, unfortunately became refractory on their passage, and very sensibly refused, when the bridge was about to give way, to proceed any further; consequently when the downfall of the arches took place the basket men remained very quietly on that part of the bridge which was left standing, and instead of being consigned to the waves had nearly been set on fire. The audience, not giving the troops due credit for their prudence, found no little fault with their compliance with the law of self-preservation. In the following representations of the opera the bridge and basket men which, *en passant* (or *en restant* rather), had cost fifty pounds, were omitted."[1] When "Moïse" was

[1] *Op. cit.*, p. 160.

prepared in Paris 45,000 francs were sunk in the Red Sea.

I shall recur in a moment to the famous *preghiera* but, having Ebers' book before me, I see an anecdote so delightfully illustrative of the proverbial spirit of the lyric theatre that I cannot resist the temptation to repeat it. In the revised "Moses" made for Paris there occurs a quartet beginning "Mi manca la voce" ("I lack voice") which Chorley describes as "a delicious round." Camporese had to utter the words first and no sooner had she done so than Ronzi di Begnis, in a whisper, loud enough to be heard by her companion, made the comment "E vero !" ("True !") — "a remark," says Mr. Ebers, "which produced a retort courteous somewhat more than verging on the limit of decorum, though not proceeding to the extremity asserted by rumor, which would have been as inconsistent with propriety as with the habitual dignity and self-possession of Camporese's demeanor."

Somebody, I cannot recall who, has said that the success of "Dal tuo stellato" set the fashion of introducing prayers into operas. Whether this be true or not, it is a fact that a prayer occurs in four of the operas which Rossini composed for the Paris Grand Opéra and that the formula is become so common that it may be set down as an operatic convention, — a convention, moreover, which even the iconoclast Wagner left undisturbed. One might think that the propriety of prayer in a religious drama would have been enforced upon the mind of a classicist like Goethe by his admiration for the antique, but it was the fact that Rossini's opera showed the Israelites upon their knees in supplication to God that set the great German poet against "Mosè." In a conversation recorded by Eckermann as taking place in 1828, we hear him uttering his objection to the work: "I do not understand how you can separate and enjoy separately the subject and the music. You pretend here that the subject is worthless, but you are consoled for it by a feast of excellent music. I wonder that your nature is thus organized that your ear can listen to charming sounds while your sight, the most perfect of your senses, is tormented by absurd objects. You will not deny that your 'Moses' is in effect very absurd. The curtain is raised and people are praying. This is all wrong. The Bible says that when you pray you should go into your chamber and close the door. Therefore, there should be no praying in the theatre. As for me, I should have arranged a wholly different 'Moses.' At first I should have shown the children of Israel bowed down by countless odious burdens and suffering from the tyranny of the Egyptian rulers. Then you would have appreciated more easily what Moses deserved from his race, which he had delivered from a shameful oppression." "Then," says Mr. Philip Hale, who directed my attention to this interesting passage, "Goethe went on to

c

reconstruct the whole opera. He introduced, for instance, a dance of the Egyptians after the plague of darkness was dispelled."

May not one criticise Goethe? If he so greatly reverenced prayer, according to its institution under the New Dispensation, why did he not show regard also for the Old and respect the verities of history sufficiently to reserve his ballet till after the passage of the Red Sea, when Moses celebrated the miracle with a song and "Miriam, the prophetess, the sister of Aaron, took a timbrel in her hand; and all the women went out after her with timbrels and with dances"?

CHAPTER II

BIBLE STORIES IN OPERA AND ORATORIO

It was the fond belief of Dr. Chrysander, born of his deep devotion to Handel, in whose works he lived and moved and had his being, that the heroic histories of the Jews offered no fit material for dramatic representation. In his view the Jews never created dramatic poetry, partly because of the Mosaic prohibition against plastic delineation of their Deity, partly because the tragic element, which was so potent an influence in the development of the Greek drama, was wanting in their heroes. The theory that the Song of Songs, that canticle of canticles of love, was a pastoral play had no lodgment in his mind; the poem seemed less dramatic to him than the Book of Job. The former sprang from the idyllic life of the northern tribes and reflected that life; the latter, much more profound in conception, proved by its form that the road to a real stage-play was insurmountably barred to the Hebrew poet. What poetic field was open to him then? Only the hymning of a Deity, invisible, omnipresent and omnipotent, the swelling call to combat for the glory of God against an inimical world, and the celebration of an ideal consisting in

19

a peaceful, happy existence in the Land of Promise under God's protecting care. This God presented Himself occasionally as a militant, all-powerful warrior, but only in moments when the fortunes of His people were critically at issue. These moments, however, were exceptional and few; as a rule, God manifested Himself in prophecy, through words and music. The laws were promulgated in song; so were the prophetic promises, denunciations, and calls to repentance; and there grew up a magnificent liturgical service in the temple.

Hebrew poetry, epic and lyrical, was thus antagonistic to the drama. So, also, Dr. Chrysander contends, was the Hebrew himself. Not only had he no predilection for plastic creation, his life was not dramatic in the sense illustrated in Greek tragedy. He lived a care-free, sensuous existence, and either fell under righteous condemnation for his transgressions or walked in the way prescribed of the Lord and found rest at last in Abraham's bosom. His life was simple; so were his strivings, his longings, his hopes. Yet when it came to the defence or celebration of his spiritual possessions his soul was filled with such a spirit of heroic daring, such a glow of enthusiasm, as are not to be paralleled among another of the peoples of antiquity. He thus became a fit subject for only one of the arts — music; in this art for only one of its spheres, the sublime, the most appropriate and efficient vehicle of which is the oratorio.

One part of this argument seems to me irrelevant; the other not firmly founded in fact. It does not follow that because the Greek conscience evolved the conceptions of rebellious pride and punitive Fate while the Hebrew conscience did not, therefore the Greeks were the predestined creators of the art-form out of which grew the opera and the Hebrews of the form which grew into the oratorio. Neither is it true that because a people are not disposed toward dramatic creation themselves they can not, or may not, be the cause of dramatic creativeness in others. Dr. Chrysander's argument, made in a lecture at the Johanneum in Hamburg in 1896, preceded an analysis of Handel's Biblical oratorios in their relation to Hebrew history, and his exposition of that history as he unfolded it chronologically from the Exodus down to the Maccabæan period was in itself sufficient to furnish many more fit operatic plots than have yet been written. Nor are there lacking in these stories some of the elements of Greek legend and mythology which were the mainsprings of the tragedies of Athens. The parallels are striking: Jephtha's daughter and Iphigenia; Samson and his slavery and the servitude of Hercules and Perseus; the fate of Ajax and other heroes made mad by pride, and the lycanthropy of Nebuchadnezzar, of whose vanity Dr. Hanslick once reminded Wagner, warning him against the fate of the Babylonian king who became like unto an ox, "ate grass and was composed by Verdi"; think reverently of Alcestis and the Christian doctrine of atonement !

The writers of the first Biblical operas sought their subjects as far back in history, or legend, as the written page permitted. Theile composed an "Adam and Eve" in 1678; but our first parents never became popular on the serious stage. Perhaps the fearful soul of the theatrical costumer was frightened and perplexed by the problem which the subject put up to him. Haydn introduced them into his oratorio "The Creation," but, as the custom goes now, the third part of the work, in which they appear, is frequently, if not generally omitted in performance. Adam, to judge by the record in Holy Writ, made an uneventful end: "And all the days that Adam lived were nine hundred and thirty years: and he died"; but this did not prevent Lesueur from writing an opera on his death ten years after Haydn's oratorio had its first performance. He called it "La Mort d'Adam et son Apothéose," and it involved him in a disastrous quarrel with the directors of the Conservatoire and the Académie. Pursuing the search chronologically, the librettists next came upon Cain and Abel, who offered a more fruitful subject for dramatic and musical invention. We know very little about the sacred operas which shared the list with works based on classical fables and Roman history in the seventeenth and eighteenth centuries; inasmuch, however, as they were an outgrowth of the pious plays of the Middle Ages and designed for edifying consumption in Lent, it is likely that they adhered in their plots pretty close to the Biblical accounts. I doubt if the sentimental element which was in vogue when Rossini wrote "Mosè in Egitto" played much of a rôle in such an opera as Johann Philipp Förtsch's "Kain und Abel; oder der verzweifelnde Brudermörder," which was performed in Hamburg in 1689, or even in "Abel's Tod," which came along in 1771. The first fratricidal murder seems to have had an early and an enduring fascination for dramatic poets and composers. Metastasio's "La Morte d'Abele," set by both Caldara and Leo in 1732, remained a stalking-horse for composers down to Morlacchi in 1820. One of the latest of Biblical operas is the "Kain" of Heinrich Bulthaupt and Eugen d'Albert. This opera and a later lyric drama by the same composer, "Tote Augen" (under which title a casual reader would never suspect that a Biblical subject was lurking), call for a little attention because of their indication of a possible drift which future dramatists may follow in treating sacred story.

Wicked envy and jealousy were not sufficient motives in the eyes of Bulthaupt and d'Albert for the first fratricide; there must be an infusion of psychology and modern philosophy. *Abel* is an optimist, an idealist, a contented dreamer, joying in the loveliness of life and nature; *Cain*, a pessimist, a morose brooder, for whom life contained no beautiful illusions. He gets up from his couch in the night to question the right of God to create man for suffering. He is answered by *Lucifer*, who proclaims himself the benefactor of the family in having rescued them from the slothful existence of Eden and given them a Redeemer. The devil discourses on the delightful ministrations of that Redeemer, whose name is Death. In the morning *Abel* arises and as he offers his sacrifice he hymns the sacred mystery of life and turns a deaf ear to the newfound gospel of his brother. An inspiring thought comes to *Cain;* by killing *Abel* and destroying himself he will save future generations from the sufferings to which they are doomed. With this benevolent purpose in mind he commits the murder. The blow has scarcely been struck before a multitude of spirit-voices call his name and God thunders the question: "Where is Abel, thy brother?" *Adam* comes from his cave and looks upon the scene with horror. Now *Cain* realizes that his work is less than half done: he is himself still alive and so is his son *Enoch.* He rushes forward to kill his child, but the mother throws herself between, and *Cain* discovers that he is not strongwilled enough to carry out his design. God's curse condemns him to eternal unrest, and while the elements rage around him *Cain* goes forth into the mountain wilderness.

Herr Bulthaupt did not permit chronology to stand in the way of his action, but it can at least be said for him that he did not profane the Book as Herr Ewers, Mr. d'Albert's latest collaborator, did when he turned a story of Christ's miraculous healing of a blind woman into a sensational melodrama. In the precious opera, "Tote Augen" ("Dead Eyes"), brought out in March, 1916, in Dresden, *Myrocle*, the blind woman, is the wife of *Arcesius*, a Roman ambassador in Jerusalem. Never having seen him, *Myrocle* believes her husband to be a paragon of beauty, but he is, in fact, hideous of features, crook-backed, and lame; deformed in mind and heart, too, for he has concealed the truth from her. *Christ* is entering Jerusalem, and *Mary of Magdala* leads *Myrocle* to him, having heard of the miracles which he performs, and he opens the woman's eyes at the moment that the multitude is shouting its hosannahs. The first man who fills the vision of *Myrocle* is *Galba*, handsome, noble, chivalrous, who had renounced the love he bore her because she was the wife of his friend. In *Galba* the woman believes she sees the husband whom in her fond imagination she had fitted out with the charms of mind and person which his friend possesses. She throws herself into his arms, and he does not repel her mistaken embraces; but the misshapen villain throws himself upon the pair and strangles his friend to death. A slave enlightens the mystified woman; the murderer, not the dead hero at his feet, is her husband. Singularly enough, she does not turn from him with hatred and loathing, but looks upon him with a great pity. Then she turns her eyes upon the sun, which *Christ* had said should not set until she had cursed him, and gazes into its searing glow until her sight is again dead.   Moral : it is sinful to love the loveliness of outward things; from the soul must come salvation.   As if she had never learned the truth, she returns to her wifely love for *Arcesius*.   The story is as false to nature as it is sacrilegious ; its trumpery theatricalism is as great a hindrance to a possible return of Biblical opera as the disgusting celebration of necrophilism in Richard Strauss's "Salome."

In our historical excursion we are still among the patriarchs, and the whole earth is of one language and of one speech.   Noah, the ark, and the deluge seem now too prodigious to be essayed by opera makers, but, apparently, they did not awe the Englishman Edward Eccleston (or Eggleston), who is said to have produced an opera, "Noah's Flood, or the Destruction of the World," in London in 1679, nor Seyfried, whose "Libera me" was sung at Beethoven's funeral, and who, besides Biblical operas entitled "Saul," "Abraham," "The Maccabees," and "The Israelites in the Desert," brought out a "Noah" in Vienna in 1818.   Halévy left an unfinished opera, "Noé," which Bizet, who was his son-in-law, completed.   Of oratorios dealing with the deluge I do not wish to speak further than to express my admiration for the manner in which Saint-Saëns opened the musical floodgates in "Le Déluge."

On the plain in the Land of Shinar the families of the sons of Noah builded them a city and a tower whose top they arrogantly hoped might reach unto heaven. But the tower fell, the tongues of the people were confounded, and the people were scattered abroad on the face of the earth. Rubinstein attempted to give dramatic representation to the tremendous incident, and to his effort and vain dream I shall revert in the next chapter of this book. Now I must on with the history of the patriarchs. The story of Abraham and his attempted offering of Isaac has been much used as oratorio material, and Joseph Elsner, Chopin's teacher, brought out a Polish opera, "Ofiara Abrama," at Warsaw in 1827.

A significant milestone in the history of the Hebrews as well as Biblical operas has now been reached. The sojourn of the Jews in Egypt and their final departure under the guidance of Moses have already occupied considerable attention in this study. They provided material for the two operas which seem to me the noblest of their kind — Méhul's "Joseph" and Rossini's "Mosè in Egitto." Méhul's opera, more than a decade older than Rossini's, still holds a place on the stages of France and Germany, and this despite the fact that it foregoes two factors which are popularly supposed to be essential to operatic success — a love episode and woman's presence and participation in the action. The opera, which is in three acts, was brought forward at the Théâtre Feydeau in Paris on February 17, 1807. It owed its origin to a Biblical tragedy entitled "Omasis," by Baour Lormian. The subject — the sale of Joseph by his brothers into Egyptian slavery, his rise to power, his forgiveness of the wrong attempted against him, and his provision of a home for the people of Israel in the land of Goshen — had long been popular with composers of oratorios. The list of these works begins with Caldara's "Giuseppe" in 1722. Metastasio's "Giuseppe riconosciuto" was set by half a dozen composers between 1733 and 1788. Handel wrote his English oratorio in 1743; G. A. Macfarren's was performed at the Leeds festival of 1877. Lormian thought it necessary to introduce a love episode into his tragedy, but Alexander Duval, who wrote the book for Méhul's opera, was of the opinion that the diversion only enfeebled the beautiful if austere picture of patriarchal domestic life delineated in the Bible. He therefore adhered to tradition and created a series of scenes full of beauty, dignity, and pathos, simple and strong in spite of the bombast prevalent in the literary style of the period. Méhul's music is marked by grandeur, simplicity, lofty sentiment, and consistent severity of manner. The composer's predilection for ecclesiastical music, created, no doubt, by the blind organist who taught him in his childhood and nourished by his studies and labors at the monastery under the gifted Hauser, found

opportunity for expression in the religious sentiments of the drama, and his knowledge of plain
chant is exhibited in the score "the simplicity,
grandeur, and dramatic truth of which will always
command the admiration of impartial musicians,"
remarks Gustave Choquet. The enthusiasm of M.
Tiersot goes further still, for he says that the music
of "Joseph" is more conspicuous for the qualities
of dignity and sonority than that of Handel's
oratorio. The German Hanslick, to whom the absence from the action of the "salt of the earth,
women" seemed disastrous, nevertheless does not
hesitate to institute a comparison between "Joseph"
and one of Mozart's latest operas. "In its mild,
passionless benevolence the entire rôle of Joseph in
Méhul's opera," he says, "reminds one strikingly
of Mozart's 'Titus,' and not to the advantage of
the latter. The opera 'Titus' is the work of an
incomparably greater genius, but it belongs to a
partly untruthful, wholly modish, tendency (that
of the old *opera seria*), while the genre of 'Joseph'
is thoroughly noble, true, and eminently dramatic.
'Joseph' has outlived 'Titus.'" [1] Carl Maria von
Weber admired Méhul's opera greatly, and within
recent years Felix Weingartner has edited a German
edition for which he composed recitatives to take
the place of the spoken dialogue of the original book.

There is no story of passion in "Joseph." The
love portrayed there is domestic and filial; its

[1] "Die Moderne Opera," p. 92.

objects are the hero's father, brothers, and country — "Champs eternels, Hebron, douce vallée." It was not until our own day that an author with a perverted sense which had already found gratification in the stench of mental, moral, and physical decay exhaled by "Salome" and "Elektra" nosed the piquant, pungent odor of the episode of Potiphar's wife and blew it into the theatre. Joseph's temptress did not tempt even the prurient taste which gave us the Parisian operatic versions of the stories of Phryne, Thaïs and Messalina. Richard Strauss's "Josephslegende" stands alone in musical literature. There is, indeed, only one reference in the records of oratorio or opera to the woman whose grovelling carnality is made the foil of Joseph's virtue in the story as told in the Book. That reference is found in a singular trilogy, which was obviously written more to disclose the possibilities of counterpoint than to set forth the story — even if it does that, which I cannot say; the suggestion comes only from a title. In August, 1852, Pietro Raimondi produced an oratorio in three parts entitled, respectively, "Putifar," "Giuseppe giusto" and "Giacobbe," at the Teatro Argentina, in Rome. The music of the three works was so written that after each had been performed separately, with individual principal singers, choristers, and orchestras, they were united in a simultaneous performance. The success of the stupendous experiment in contrapuntal writing was so great that the composer fell in a faint amidst the applause of the audience and died less than three months afterward.

In the course of this study I have mentioned nearly all of the Biblical characters who have been turned into operatic heroes. Nebuchadnezzar appeared on the stage at Hamburg in an opera of Keiser's in 1704; Ariosti put him through his bovine strides in Vienna in 1706. He was put into a ballet by a Portuguese composer and made the butt of a French opéra bouffe writer, J. J. Debillement, in 1871. He recurs to my mind now in connection with a witty fling at "Nabucco" made by a French rhymester when Verdi's opera was produced at Paris in 1845. The noisy brass in the orchestration offended the ears of a critic, and he wrote:

> Vraiment l'affiche est dans son tort;
>   En faux, ou devrait la poursuivre.
> Pourquoi nous annoncer Nabuchodonos — or
>   Quand c'est Nabuchodonos — cuivre?

Judas Maccabæus is one of the few heroes of ancient Israel who have survived in opera, Rubinstein's "Makkabäer" still having a hold, though not a strong one, on the German stage. The libretto is an adaptation by Mosenthal (author also of Goldmark's "Queen of Sheba") of a drama by Otto Ludwig. In the drama as well as some of its predecessors some liberties have been taken with the story as told in Maccabees II, chapter 7. The tale of the Israelitish champion of freedom and his brothers Jonathan and Simon, who lost their lives in the struggle against the tyranny of the kings of Syria, is intensely dramatic. For stage purposes the dramatists have associated the massacre of a mother and her seven sons and the martyrdom of the aged Eleazar, who caused the uprising of the Jews, with the family history of Judas himself. J. W. Franck produced "Die Maccabäische Mutter" in Hamburg in 1679, Ariosti composed "La Madre dei Maccabei" in 1704, Ignaz von Seyfried brought out "Die Makkabäer, oder Salmonäa" in 1818, and Rubinstein his opera in Berlin on April 17, 1875.

The romantic career of Jephtha, a natural son, banished from home, chief of a band of roving marauders, mighty captain and ninth judge of Israel, might have fitted out many an opera text, irrespective of the pathetic story of the sacrifice of his daughter in obedience to a vow, though this episode springs first to mind when his name is mentioned, and has been the special subject of the Jephtha operas. An Italian composer named Pollarolo wrote a "Jefte" for Vienna in 1692; other operas dealing with the history are Rolle's "Mehala, die Tochter Jephthas" (1784), Meyerbeer's "Jephtha's Tochter" (Munich, 1813), Generali, "Il voto di Jefte" (1827), Sanpieri, "La Figlia di Jefte" (1872). Luis Cepeda produced a Spanish opera in Madrid in 1845, and a French opera, in five acts and a prologue, by Monteclaire, was prohibited, after one performance, by Cardinal de Noailles in 1832.

Judith, the widow of Manasseh, who delivered her native city of Bethulia from the Assyrian Holofernes, lulling him to sleep with her charms and then striking off his drunken head with a falchion, though an Apocryphal personage, is the most popular of Israelitish heroines. The record shows the operas "Judith und Holofernes" by Leopold Kotzeluch (1799), "Giuditta" by S. Levi (1844), Achille Peri (1860), Righi (1871), and Sarri (1875). Naumann wrote a "Judith" in 1858, Doppler another in 1870, and Alexander Seroff a Russian opera under the same title in 1863. Martin Röder, who used to live in Boston, composed a "Judith," but it was never performed, while George W. Chadwick's "Judith," half cantata, half opera, which might easily be fitted for the stage, has had to rest content with a concert performance at a Worcester (Mass.) festival.

The memory of Esther, the queen of Ahasuerus, who saved her people from massacre, is preserved and her deed celebrated by the Jews in their gracious festival of Purim. A gorgeous figure for the stage, she has been relegated to the oratorio platform since the end of the eighteenth century. Racine's tragedy "Athalie" has called out music from Abbé Vogler, Gossec, Boïeldieu, Mendelssohn, and others, and a few oratorios, one by Handel, have been based on the story of the woman through whom idolatry was introduced into Judah; but I have no record of any Athalia opera.

D

CHAPTER III

I HAVE a strong belief in the essential excellence
of Biblical subjects for the purposes of the lyric
drama — at least from an historical point of view.
I can see no reason against but many reasons in
favor of a return to the stage of the patriarchal
and heroic figures of the people who are a more
potent power in the world to-day, despite their
dispersal and loss of national unity, than they were
in the days of their political grandeur and glory.
Throughout the greater part of his creative career
Anton Rubinstein was the champion of a similar
idea. Of the twenty works which he wrote for the
theatre, including ballets, six were on Biblical
subjects, and to promote a propaganda which
began with the composition of "Der Thurmbau
zu Babel," in 1870, he not only entered the literary
field, but made personal appeal for practical assist-
ance in both the Old World and the New. His,
however, was a religious point of view, not the historical or political. It is very likely that a racial
predilection had much to do with his attitude on
the subject, but in his effort to bring religion into

34

the service of the lyric stage he was no more Jew than Christian : the stories to which he applied his greatest energies were those of Moses and Christ.

Much against my inclination (for Rubinstein came into my intellectual life under circumstances and conditions which made him the strongest personal influence in music that I have ever felt) I have been compelled to believe that there were other reasons besides those which he gave for his championship of Biblical opera. Smaller men than he, since Wagner's death, have written trilogies and dreamed of theatres and festivals devoted to performances of their works. Little wonder if Rubinstein believed that he had created, or could create, a kind of art-work which should take place by the side of "Der Ring des Nibelungen," and have its special home like Bayreuth ; and it may have been a belief that his project would excite the sympathetic zeal of the devout Jew and pious Christian alike, as much as his lack of the capacity for self-criticism, which led him like a will-o'-the-wisp along the path which led into the bogs of failure and disappointment.

While I was engaged in writing the programme book for the music festival given in New York in 1881, at which "The Tower of Babel" was performed in a truly magnificent manner, Dr. Leopold Damrosch, the conductor of the festival, told me that Rubinstein had told him that the impulse to use Biblical subjects in lyrical dramas had come to him while witnessing a ballet based on a Bible story many years before in Paris. He said that he had seldom been moved so profoundly by any spectacle as by this ballet, and it suggested to him the propriety of treating sacred subjects in a manner worthy of them, yet different from the conventional oratorio. The explanation has not gotten into the books, but is not inconsistent with the genesis of his Biblical operas, as related by Rubinstein in his essay on the subject printed by Joseph Lewinsky in his book "Vor den Coulissen," published in 1882 after at least three of the operas had been written. The composer's defence of his works and his story of the effort which he made to bring about a realization of his ideals deserve to be rehearsed in justice to his character as man and artist, as well as in the interest of the works themselves and the subjects, which, I believe, will in the near future occupy the minds of composers again.

"The oratorio," said Rubinstein, "is an art-form which I have always been disposed to protest against. The best-known masterpieces of this form have, not during the study of them but when hearing them performed, always left me cold; indeed, often positively pained me. The stiffness of the musical and still more of the poetical form always seemed to me absolutely incongruous with the high dramatic feeling of the subject. To see and hear gentlemen in dress coats, white cravats, yellow gloves, holding music books before them,

or ladies in modern, often extravagant, toilets singing the parts of the grand, imposing figures of the
Old and New Testaments has always disturbed
me to such a degree that I could never attain to
pure enjoyment. Involuntarily I felt and thought
how much grander, more impressive, vivid, and
true would be all that I had experienced in the
concert-room if represented on the stage with costumes, decorations, and full action."

The contention, said Rubinstein in effect, that
Biblical subjects are ill adapted to the stage because of their sacred character is a testimony of
poverty for the theatre, which should be an agency
in the service of the highest purposes of culture.
The people have always wanted to see stage representations of Bible incidents; witness the mystery
plays of the Middle Ages and the Passion Play at
Oberammergau to-day. But yielding to a prevalent feeling that such representations are a profanation of sacred history, he had conceived an
appropriate type of art-work which was to be produced in theatres to be specially built for the purpose
and by companies of artists to be specially trained
to that end. This art-work was to be called Sacred
Opera (*geistliche Oper*), to distinguish it from secular
opera, but its purpose was to be purely artistic and
wholly separate from the interests of the Church.
He developed ways and means for raising the necessary funds, enlisting artists, overcoming the difficulties presented by the *mise en scène* and the

polyphonic character of the choral music, and set
forth his aim in respect of the subject-matter of the
dramas to be a representation in chronological
order of the chief incidents described in the Old
and New Testaments. He would be willing to
include in his scheme Biblical operas already existing, if they were not all, with the exception of
Méhul's "Joseph," made unfit by their treatment
of sacred matters, especially by their inclusion of
love episodes which brought them into the domain
of secular opera.

For years, while on his concert tours in various
countries, Rubinstein labored to put his plan into
operation. Wherever he found a public accustomed to oratorio performances he inquired into
the possibility of establishing his sacred theatre
there. He laid the project before the Grand Duke
of Weimar, who told him that it was feasible only
in large cities. The advice sent him to Berlin,
where he opened his mind to the Minister of Education, von Mühler. The official had his doubts;
sacred operas might do for Old Testament stories,
but not for New; moreover, such a theatre should
be a private, not a governmental, undertaking.
He sought the opinion of Stanley, Dean of West-
minster Abbey, who said that he could only conceive a realization of the idea in the oldtime popular
manner, upon a rude stage at a country fair.

For a space it looked as if the leaders of the
Jewish congregations in Paris would provide funds

for the enterprise so far as it concerned itself with subjects taken from the Old Dispensation; but at the last they backed out, fearing to take the initiative in a matter likely to cause popular clamor. "I even thought of America," says Rubinstein, "of the daring transatlantic impresarios, with their lust of enterprise, who might be inclined to speculate on a gigantic scale with my idea. I had indeed almost succeeded, but the lack of artists brought it to pass that the plans, already in a considerable degree of forwardness, had to be abandoned. I considered the possibility of forming an association of composers and performing artists to work together to carry on the enterprise materially, intellectually, and administratively; but the great difficulty of enlisting any considerable number of artists for the furtherance of a new idea in art frightened me back from this purpose also." In these schemes there are evidences of Rubinstein's willingness to follow examples set by Handel as well as Wagner. The former composed "Judas Maccabæus" and "Alexander Balus" to please the Jews who had come to his help when he made financial shipwreck with his opera; the latter created the Richard Wagner Verein to put the Bayreuth enterprise on its feet.

Of the six sacred operas composed by Rubinstein three may be said to be practicable for stage representation. They are "Die Makkabäer," "Sulamith" (based on Solomon's Song of Songs) and

"Christus." The first has had many performances in Germany; the second had a few performances in Hamburg in 1883; the last, first performed as an oratorio in Berlin in 1885, was staged in Bremen in 1895. It has had, I believe, about fourteen representations in all. As for the other three works, "Der Thurmbau zu Babel" (first performance in Königsberg in 1870), "Das verlorene Paradies" (Düsseldorf, 1875), and "Moses" (still awaiting theatrical representation, I believe), it may be said of them that they are hybrid creations which combine the oratorio and opera styles by utilizing the powers of the oldtime oratorio chorus and the modern orchestra, with the descriptive capacity of both raised to the highest power, to illustrate an action which is beyond the capabilities of the ordinary stage machinery. In the character of the forms employed in the works there is no startling innovation; we meet the same alternation of chorus, recitative, aria, and *ensemble* that we have known since the oratorio style was perfected. A change, however, has come over the spirit of the expression and the forms have all relaxed some of their rigidity. In the oratorios of Handel and Haydn there are instances not a few of musical delineation in the instrumental as well as the vocal parts; but nothing in them can be thought of, so far at least as the ambition of the design extends, as a companion piece to the scene in the opera which pictures the destruction of the tower of Babel. This is as far

beyond the horizon of the fancy of the old masters
as it is beyond the instrumental forces which they
controlled.

"Paradise Lost," the text paraphrased from
portions of Milton's epic, is an oratorio pure and
simple. It deals with the creation of the world
according to the Mosaic (or as Huxley would have
said, Miltonic) theory and the medium of expression is an alternation of recitatives and choruses,
the latter having some dramatic life and a characteristic accompaniment. It is wholly contem-
plative; there is nothing like action in it. "The
Tower of Babel" has action in the restricted sense
in which it enters into Mendelssohn's oratorios,
and scenic effects which would tax the utmost
powers of the modern stage-machinist who might
attempt to carry them out. A mimic tower of
Babel is more preposterous than a mimic temple
of Dagon; yet, unless Rubinstein's stage directions
are to be taken in a Pickwickian sense, we ought
to listen to this music while looking at a stage-setting
more colossal than any ever contemplated by dramatist before. We should see a wide stretch of the
plain of Shinar; in the foreground a tower so tall
as to give color of plausibility to a speech which
prates of an early piercing of heaven and so large
as to provide room for a sleeping multitude on its
scaffoldings. Brick kilns, derricks, and all the apparatus and machinery of building should be on all
hands, and from the summit of a mound should

grow a giant tree, against whose trunk should hang a brazen shield to be used as a signal gong. We should see in the progress of the opera the bustling activity of the workmen, the roaring flames and rolling smoke of the brick kilns, and witness the miraculous spectacle of a man thrown into the fire and walking thence unharmed. We should see (in dissolving views) the dispersion of the races and behold the unfolding of a rainbow in the sky. And, finally, we should get a glimpse of an open heaven and the Almighty on His throne, and a yawning hell, with Satan and his angels exercising their dread dominion. Can such scenes be mimicked successfully enough to preserve a serious frame of mind in the observer? Hardly. Yet the music seems obviously to have been written in the expectation that sight shall aid hearing to quicken the fancy and emotion and excite the faculties to an appreciation of the work.

"The Tower of Babel" has been performed upon the stage; how I cannot even guess. Knowing, probably, that the work would be given in concert form oftener than in dramatic, Rubinstein tries to stimulate the fancy of those who must be only listeners by profuse stage directions which are printed in the score as well as the book of words. "Moses" is in the same case. By the time that Rubinstein had completed it he evidently realized that its hybrid character as well as its stupendous scope would stand in the way of performances of

any kind. Before even a portion of its music
had been heard in public, he wrote in a letter to a
friend: "It is too theatrical for the concert-room
and too much like an oratorio for the theatre. It
is, in fact, the perfect type of the sacred opera that
I have dreamed of for years. What will come of
it I do not know; I do not think it can be performed
entire. As it contains eight distinct parts, one or
two may from time to time be given either in a
concert or on the stage."

America was the first country to act on the suggestion of a fragmentary performance. The first
scene was brought forward in New York by Walter
Damrosch at a public rehearsal and concert of the
Symphony Society (the Oratorio Society assisting)
on January 18 and 19, 1889. The third scene was
performed by the German Liederkranz, under
Reinhold L. Herman, on January 27 of the same
year. The third and fourth scenes were in the
scheme of the Cincinnati Music Festival, Theodore
Thomas, conductor, on May 25, 1894.

Each of the eight scenes into which the work is
divided deals with an episode in the life of Israel's
lawgiver. In the first scene we have the incident
of the finding of the child in the bulrushes; in the
second occurs the oppression of the *Israelites* by
the Egyptian taskmasters, the slaying of one of the
overseers by *Moses*, who, till then regarded as the
king's son, now proclaims himself one of the oppressed race. The third scene discloses *Moses*

protecting *Zipporah*, daughter of *Jethro*, a Midianit-
ish priest, from a band of marauding Edomites,
his acceptance of *Jethro's* hospitality and the scene
of the burning bush and the proclamation of his
mission. Scene IV deals with the plagues, those of
blood, hail, locusts, frogs, and vermin being delineated
in the instrumental introduction to the part, the
action beginning while the land is shrouded in the
"thick darkness that might be felt." The *Egyptians* call upon Osiris to dispel the darkness, but
are forced at last to appeal to *Moses*. He demands
the liberation of his people as the price to be paid
for the removal of the plague; receiving a promise
from *Pharaoh*, he utters a prayer ending with "Let
there be light." The result is celebrated in a brilliant choral acclamation of the returning sun. The
scene has a parallel in Rossini's opera. *Pharaoh* now
equivocates; he will free the sons of Jacob, but not
the women, children, or chattels. *Moses* threatens
punishment in the death of all of Egypt's first-
born, and immediately solo and chorus voices be-
wail the new affliction. When the king hears that
his son is dead he gives his consent, and the *Israelites*
depart with an ejaculation of thanks to Jehovah.
The passage of the Red Sea, *Miriam's* celebration
of that miracle, the backsliding of the *Israelites*
and their worship of the golden calf, the reception
of the Tables of the Law, the battle between the
Israelites and *Moabites* on the threshold of the
Promised Land, and the evanishment and apotheosis

of *Moses* are the contents of the remainder of the
work.

*

*   *

It is scarcely to be wondered at that the subjects
which opera composers have found adaptable to
their uses in the New Testament are very few compared with those offered by the Old. The books
written by the evangelists around the most stupendous tragical story of all time set forth little or
nothing (outside of the birth, childhood, teachings,
miracles, death, and resurrection of Jesus of Nazareth)
which could by any literary ingenuity be turned into
a stage play except the parables with which Christ
enforced and illustrated His sermons. The sublime
language and imagery of the Apocalypse have fur-
nished forth the textual body of many oratorios, but
it still transcends the capacity of mortal dramatist.

In the parable of the Prodigal Son there is no
personage whose presentation in dramatic garb
could be looked upon as a profanation of the Scrip-
tures. It is this fact, probably, coupled with its
profoundly beautiful reflection of human nature,
which has made it a popular subject with opera
writers. There was an Italian "Figliuolo Prodigo" as early as 1704, composed by one Biffi; a
French melodrama, "L'Enfant Prodigue," by Mo-
range about 1810; a German piece of similar character by Joseph Drechsler in Vienna in 1820. Pierre
Gaveaux, who composed "Léonore, ou l'Amour

Conjugal," which provided Beethoven with his "Fidelio," brought out a comic opera on the subject of the Prodigal Son in 1811, and Berton, who had also dipped into Old Testament story in an oratorio, entitled "Absalon," illustrated the parable in a ballet. The most recent settings of the theme are also the most significant: Auber's five-act opera "L'Enfant Prodigue," brought out in Paris in 1850, and Ponchielli's "Il Figliuolo Prodigo," in four acts, which had its first representation at La Scala in 1880.

The mediæval mysteries were frequently interspersed with choral songs, for which the liturgy of the Church provided material. If we choose to look upon them as incipient operas or precursors of that art-form we must yet observe that their monkish authors, willing enough to trick out the story of the Nativity with legendary matter drawn from the Apocryphal New Testament, which discloses anything but a reverential attitude toward the sublime tragedy, nevertheless stood in such awe before the spectacle of Calvary that they deemed it wise to leave its dramatic treatment to the church service in the Passion Tide. In that service there was something approaching to characterization in the manner of the reading by the three deacons appointed to deliver, respectively, the narrative, the words of Christ, and the utterances of the Apostles and people; and it may be that this and the liturgical solemnities of Holy Week were reverently thought sufficient by them and the authors of the first sacred operas. Nevertheless, we have Keiser's "Der Blutige und Sterbende Jesus," performed at Hamburg, and Metastasio's "La Passione di Gesù Christi," composed first by Caldara, which probably was an oratorio.

Earlier than these was Theile's "Die Geburt Christi," performed in Hamburg in 1681. The birth of Christ and His childhood (there was an operatic representation of His presentation in the Temple) were subjects which appealed more to the writers of the rude plays which catered to the popular love for dramatic mummery than did His crucifixion. I am speaking now more specifically of lyric dramas, but it is worthy of note that in the Coventry mysteries, as Hone points out in the preface to his book, "Ancient Mysteries Described," [1] there are eight plays, or pageants, which deal with the Nativity as related in the canon and the pseudo-gospels. In them much stress was laid upon the suspicions of the Virgin Mother's chastity, for here was material that was good for rude diversion as well as instruction in righteousness.

*

*   *

That Rubinstein dared to compose a Christ drama must be looked upon as proof of the pro-

[1] "Ancient Mysteries Described, especially the English Miracle Plays Founded on Apocryphal New Testament Story," London, 1823.

found sincerity of his belief in the art-form which he fondly hoped he had created; also, perhaps, as evidence of his artistic ingenuousness. Only a brave or naïve mind could have calmly contemplated a labor from which great dramatists, men as great as Hebbel, shrank back in alarm. After the completion of "Lohengrin" Wagner applied himself to the creation of a tragedy which he called "Jesus of Nazareth." We know his plan in detail, but he abandoned it after he had offered his sketches to a French poet as the basis of a lyric drama which he hoped to write for Paris. He confesses that he was curious to know what the Frenchman would do with a work the stage production of which would "provoke a thousand frights." He himself was unwilling to stir up such a tempest in Germany; instead, he put his sketches aside and used some of their material in his "Parsifal."

Wagner ignored the religious, or, let us say, the ecclesiastical, point of view entirely in "Jesus of Nazareth." His hero was to have been, as I have described him elsewhere,[2] "a human philosopher who preached the saving grace of Love and sought to redeem his time and people from the domination of conventional law — the offspring of selfishness. His philosophy was socialism imbued by love." Rubinstein proceeded along the lines of history, or orthodox belief, as unreservedly in his "Christus" as he had done in his "Moses." The work may be said to have brought his creative activ-

[1] "A Book of Operas," p. 288.

ities to a close, although two compositions (a set of six pianoforte pieces and an orchestral suite) appear in his list of numbered works after the sacred opera. He died on November 20, 1894, without having seen a stage representation of it. Nor did he live to see a public theatrical performance of his "Moses," though he was privileged to witness a private performance arranged at the German National Theatre in Prague so that he might form an opinion of its effectiveness. The public has never been permitted to learn anything about the impression which the work made.

On May 25, 1895, a series of representations of "Christus" was begun in Bremen, largely through the instrumentality of Professor Bulthaupt, a potent and pervasive personage in the old Hanseatic town. He was not only a poet and the author of the book of this opera and of some of Bruch's works, but also a painter, and his mural decorations in the Bremen Chamber of Commerce are proudly displayed by the citizens of the town. It was under the supervision of the painter-poet that the Bremen representations were given and, unless I am mistaken, he painted the scenery or much of it. One of the provisions of the performances was that applause was prohibited out of reverence for the sacred character of the scenes, which were as frankly set forth as at Oberammergau. The contents of the tragedy in some scenes and an epilogue briefly outlined are these : The first scene shows the temptation

E

of Christ in the wilderness, where the devil "shewed
unto him all the kingdoms of the world in a moment
of time." This disclosure is made by a series of
scenes, each opening for a short time in the background — castles, palaces, gardens, mountains of
gold, and massive heaps of earth's treasures. In the
second scene *John the Baptist* is seen and heard
preaching on the banks of the Jordan, in whose
waters he baptizes *Jesus*. This scene at the Bremen
representations was painted from sketches made
by Herr Handrich in Palestine, as was also that of
the "Sermon on the Mount" and "The Miracle
of the Loaves and Fishes," which form the subject
of the next part. The fourth tableau shows the
expulsion of the money changers from the Temple;
the fifth the Last Supper, with the garden of Geth-
semane as a background; the sixth the trial and
the last the crucifixion. Here, as if harking back
to his "Tower of Babel," Rubinstein brings in
pictures of heaven and hell, with angels and devils
contemplating the catastrophe. The proclamation
of the Gospel to the Gentiles by *St. Paul* is the subject of the epilogue.

CHAPTER IV

"SAMSON ET DALILA"

THERE are but two musical works based on the story of Samson on the current list to-day, Handel's oratorio and Saint-Saëns's opera; but lyric drama was still in its infancy when the subject first took hold of the fancy of composers and it has held it ever since. The earliest works were of the kind called sacred operas in the books and are spoken of as oratorios now, though they were doubtless performed with scenery and costumes and with action of a sort. Such were "Il Sansone" by Giovanni Paola Colonna (Bologna, 1677), "Sansone accecato da Filistri" by Francesco Antonio Uri (Venice, about 1700), "Simson" by Christoph Graupner (Hamburg, 1709), "Simson" by Georg von Pasterwitz (about 1770), "Samson" by J. N. Lefroid Mereaux (Paris, 1774), "Simson" by Johann Heinrich Rolle (about 1790), "Simson" by Franz Tuczek (Vienna, 1804), and "Il Sansone" by Francesco Basili (Naples, 1824). Two French operas are associated with great names and have interesting histories. Voltaire wrote a dramatic text on the subject at the request of La Popelinière,

51

the farmer-general, who, as poet, musician, and artist, exercised a tremendous influence in his day. Rameau was in his service as household clavecinist and set Voltaire's poem. The authors looked forward to a production on the stage of the Grand Opéra, where at least two Biblical operas, an Old Testament "Jephté" and a New Testament "Enfant prodigue" were current; but Rameau had powerful enemies, and the opera was prohibited on the eve of the day on which it was to have been performed. The composer had to stomach his mortification as best he could; he put some of his Hebrew music into the service of his Persian "Zoroastre."

The other French *Samson* to whom I have referred had also to undergo a sea-change like unto Rameau's, Rossini's *Moses*, and Verdi's *Nebuchadnezzar*. Duprez, who was ambitious to shine as a composer as well as a singer (he wrote no less than eight operas and also an oratorio, "The Last Judgment"), tried his hand on a Samson opera and succeeded in enlisting the help of Dumas the elder in writing the libretto. When he was ready to present it at the door of the Grand Opéra the Minister of Fine Arts told him that it was impracticable, as the stage-setting of the last act alone would cost more than 100,000 francs. Duprez then followed the example set with Rossini's "Mosè" in London and changed the book to make it tell a story of the crusades which he called "Zephora." Nevertheless the original form was restored in German and

Italian translations of the work, and it had concert performances in 1857. To Joachim Raff was denied even this poor comfort. He wrote a German "Simson" between 1851 and 1857. The conductor at Darmstadt to whom it was first submitted rejected it on the ground that it was too difficult for his singers. Raff then gave it to Liszt, with whom he was sojourning at Weimar, and who had taken pity on his "König Alfred"; but the tenor singer at the Weimar opera said the music was too high for the voice. Long afterward Wagner's friend, Schnorr von Carolsfeld, saw the score in the hands of the composer. The heroic stature of the hero delighted him, and his praise moved Raff to revise the opera; but before this had been done Schnorr died of the cold contracted while creating the rôle of Wagner's *Tristan* at Munich in 1865. Thus mournfully ended the third episode. As late as 1882 Raff spoke of taking the opera in hand again, but though he may have done so his death found the work unperformed and it has not yet seen the light of the stage-lamps.

Saint-Saëns's opera has also passed through many vicissitudes, but has succumbed to none and is probably possessed of more vigorous life now than it ever had. It is the recognized operatic masterpiece of the most resourceful and fecund French musician since Berlioz. Saint-Saëns began the composition of "Samson et Dalila" in 1869. The author of the book, Ferdinand Lemaire, was a cousin

of the composer. Before the breaking out of the
Franco-Prussian War the score was so far on the
way to completion that it was possible to give its
second act a private trial. This was done, an incident of the occasion — which afterward introduced one element of pathos in its history — being
the singing of the part of *Samson* by the painter
Henri Regnault, who soon after lost his life in the
service of his country. A memorial to him and
the friendship which existed between him and the
composer is the "Marche Héroique," which bears
the dead man's name on its title-page. Toward
the end of 1872 the opera was finished. For two
years the score rested in the composer's desk. Then
the second act was again brought forth for trial,
this time at the country home of Mme. Viardot,
at Croissy, the illustrious hostess singing the part of
Dalila. In 1875 the first act was performed in
concert style by M. Edouard Colonne in Paris.
Liszt interested himself in the opera and secured
its acceptance at the Grand Ducal Opera House of
Weimar, where Eduard Lassen brought it out on
December 2, 1877. Brussels heard it in 1878; but
it did not reach one of the theatres of France until
March 3, 1890, when Rouen produced it at its Thé-
âtre des Arts under the direction of M. Henri Verd-
hurt. It took nearly seven months more to reach
Paris, where the first representation was at the
Eden Theatre on October 31 of the same year.
Two years later, after it had been heard in a number

of French and Italian provincial theatres, it was given at the Académie Nationale de Musique under the direction of M. Colonne. The part of *Dalila* was taken by Mme. Deschamps-Jehin, that of *Samson* by M. Vergnet, that of the *High Priest* by M. Lassalle. Eight months before this it had been performed as an oratorio by the Oratorio Society of New York. There were two performances, on March 25 and 26, 1892, the conductor being Mr. Walter Damrosch and the principal singers being Frau Marie Ritter-Goetze, Sebastian Montariol, H. E. Distelhurst, Homer Moore, Emil Fischer, and Purdon Robinson. London had heard the work twice as an oratorio before it had a stage representation there on April 26, 1909, but this performance was fourteen years later than the first at the Metropolitan Opera House on February 8, 1895. The New York performance was scenically inadequate, but the integrity of the record demands that the cast be given here: *Samson*, Signor Tamagno; *Dalila*, Mme. Mantelli; *High Priest*, Signor Campanari; *Abimelech* and *An Old Hebrew*, M. Plançon; *First Philistine*, Signor Rinaldini; *Second Philistine*, Signor de Vachetti; conductor, Signor Mancinelli. The Metropolitan management did not venture upon a repetition until the opening night of the season 1915–1916, when its success was such that it became an active factor in the repertory of the establishment; but by that time it had been made fairly familiar to the New York public by performances at the Manhattan Opera House under the management of Mr. Oscar Hammerstein, the first of which took place on November 13, 1908. Signor Campanini conducted and the cast embraced Mme. Gerville-Réache as *Dalila*, Charles Dalmorès as *Samson*, and M. Dufranne as *High Priest*. The cast at the Metropolitan Opera House's revival of the opera on November 15, 1915, was as follows: *Dalila*, Mme. Margarete Matzenauer; *Samson*, Signor Enrico Caruso; *High Priest*, Signor Pasquale Amato; *Abimelech*, Herr Carl Schlegel; *An Old Hebrew*, M. Léon Rothier; *A Philistine Messenger*, Herr Max Bloch; *First Philistine*, Pietro Audisio; *Second Philistine*, Vincenzo Reschiglian; conductor, Signor Polacco.

*

*   *

It would be a curious inquiry to try to determine the source of the fascination which the story of Manoah's son has exerted upon mankind for centuries. It bears a likeness to the story of the son of Zeus and Alcmene, and there are few books on mythology which do not draw a parallel between the two heroes. Samson's story is singularly brief. For twenty years he "judged Israel," but the Biblical history which deals with him consists only of an account of his birth, a recital of the incidents in which he displayed his prodigious strength and valor, the tale of his amours, and, at the end, the account of his tragical destruction, brought about by the weak element in his character.

Commentators have been perplexed by the tale, irrespective of the adornments which it has received at the hands of the Talmudists. Is Samson a Hebrew form of the conception personified by the Greek Herakles? Is he a mythical creature, born in the human imagination of primitive nature worship — a variant of the Tyrian sun-god Shemesh, whose name his so curiously resembles? [1] Was he something more than a man of extraordinary physical strength and extraordinary moral weakness, whose patriotic virtues and pathetic end have kept his memory alive through the ages? Have a hundred generations of men to whom the story of Herakles has appeared to be only a fanciful romance, the product of that imagination heightened by religion which led the Greeks to exalt their supreme heroes to the extent of deification, persisted in hearing and telling the story of Samson with a sympathetic interest which betrays at least a subconscious belief in its verity? Is the story only a parable enforcing a moral lesson which is as old as humanity? If so, how got it into the canonical Book of Judges, which, with all its mythical and legendary material, seems yet to contain a large substratum of unquestionable history?

There was nothing of the divine essence in Samson as the Hebrews conceived him, except that

---

[1] In Hebrew he is called *Shimshon*, and the sun *shemesh*.

spirit of God with which he was directly endowed in supreme crises. There is little evidence of his possession of great wisdom, but strong proof of his moral and religious laxity. He sinned against the laws of Israel's God when he took a Philistine woman, an idolater, to wife; he sinned against the moral law when he visited the harlot at Gaza. He was wofully weak in character when he yielded to the blandishments of Delilah and wrought his own undoing, as well as that of his people. The disgraceful slavery into which Herakles fell was not caused by the hero's incontinence or uxoriousness, but a punishment for crime, in that he had in a fit of madness killed his friend Iphitus. And the three years which he spent as the slave of Omphale were punctuated by larger and better deeds than those of Samson in like situation — bursting the new cords with which the men of Judah had bound him and the green withes and new ropes with which Delilah shackled him. The record that Samson "judged Israel in the days of the Philistines twenty years" leads the ordinary reader to think of him as a sage, judicial personage, whereas it means only that he was the political and military leader of his people during that period, lifted to a magisterial position by his strength and prowess in war. His achievements were muscular, not mental.

Rabbinical legends have magnified his stature and power in precisely the same manner as the imagination of the poet of the "Lay of the Nibe-

lung" magnified the stature and strength of Siegfried. His shoulders, says the legend, were sixty
ells broad; when the Spirit of God came on him he
could step from Zorah to Eshtaol although he was
lame in both feet; the hairs of his head arose and
clashed against one another so that they could be
heard for a like distance; he was so strong that he
could uplift two mountains and rub them together
like two clods of earth. Herakles tore asunder
the mountain which, divided, now forms the Straits
of Gibraltar and Gates of Hercules.

The parallel which is frequently drawn between
Samson and Herakles cannot be pursued far with
advantage to the Hebrew hero. Samson rent a
young lion on the road to Timnath, whither he was
going to take his Philistine wife; Herakles, while
still a youthful herdsman, slew the Thespian lion
and afterward strangled the Nemean lion with his
hands. Samson carried off the gates of Gaza and
bore them to the top of a hill before Hebron; Herakles upheld the heavens while Atlas went to fetch
the golden apples of Hesperides. Moreover, the
feats of Herakles show a higher intellectual quality
than those of Samson, all of which, save one, were
predominantly physical. The exception was the
trick of tying 300 foxes by their tails, two by two,
with firebrands between and turning them loose to
burn the corn of the Philistines. An ingenious
way to spread a conflagration, probably, but primitive, decidedly primitive. Herakles was a scientific

engineer of the modern school; he yoked the rivers
Alpheüs and Peneüs to his service by turning their
waters through the Augean stables and cleansing
them of the deposits of 3000 oxen for thirty years.
Herakles had excellent intellectual training; Rhada-
manthus taught him wisdom and virtue, Linus
music.   We know nothing about the bringing up of
Samson save that "the child grew and the Lord
blessed him.   And the Lord began to move him at
times in the camp of Dan between Zorah and Eshtaol." Samson made little use of his musical
gifts, if he had any, but that little he made well;
Herakles made little use of his musical training,
and that little he made ill.   He lost his temper and
killed his music master with his lute; Samson, after
using an implement which only the black slaves
of our South have treated as a musical instrument,
to slay a thousand Philistines, jubilated in song: —

> With the jawbone of an ass
>   Heaps upon heaps!
> With the jawbone of an ass
>   Have I slain a thousand men!

The vast fund of human nature laid bare in the
story of Samson is, it appears to me, quite sufficient
to explain its popularity, and account for its origin.
The hero's virtues — strength, courage, patriotism
— are those which have ever won the hearts of men,
and they present themselves as but the more admirable, as they are made to appear more natural,

by pairing with that amiable weakness, susceptibility
to woman's charms.

After all Samson is a true type of the tragic hero,
whatever Dr. Chrysander or another may say.
He is impelled by Fate into a commission of the
follies which bring about the wreck of his body.
His marriage with the Philistine woman in Timnath
was part of a divine plot, though unpatriotic and
seemingly impious. When his father said unto
him : "Is there never a woman among the daughters
of thy brethren or among all my people that thou
goest to take a wife of the uncircumcised Philistines?" he did not know that "it was of the Lord
that he sought an occasion against the Philistines."
Out of that wooing and winning grew the first of
the encounters which culminated in the destruction of the temple of Dagon, when "the dead which
he slew at his death were more than they which he
slew in his life." So his yielding to the pleadings
of his wife when she betrayed the answer to his
riddle and his succumbing to the wheedling arts
of Delilah when he betrayed the secret of his strength
(acts incompatible with the character of an ordinary
strong and wise man) were of the type essential
to the machinery of the Greek drama.

A word about the mythological interpretation
of the characters which have been placed in parallel :
It may be helpful to an understanding of the Hellenic
mind to conceive Herakles as a marvellously strong
man, first glorified into a national hero and finally

deified. So, too, the theory that Herakles sinking down upon his couch of fire is but a symbol of the declining sun can be entertained without marring the grandeur of the hero or belittling Nature's phenomenon ; but it would obscure our understanding of the Hebrew intellect and profane the Hebrew religion to conceive Samson as anything but the man that the Bible says he was ; while to make of him, as Ignaz Golziher suggests, a symbol of the setting sun whose curly locks (*crines Phoebi*) are sheared by Delilah-Night, would bring contumely upon one of the most beautiful and impressive of Nature's spectacles. Before the days of comparative mythology scholars were not troubled by such interpretations. Josephus disposes of the Delilah episode curtly : "As for Samson being ensnared by a woman, that is to be ascribed to human nature, which is too weak to resist sin."

*
*   *

It is not often that an operatic figure invites to such a study as that which I have attempted in the case of Samson, and it may be that the sidewise excursion in which I have indulged invites criticism of the kind illustrated in the metaphor of using a club to brain a gnat. But I do not think so. If heroic figures seem small on the operatic stage, it is the fault of either the author or the actor. When genius in a creator is paired with genius in an interpreter, the hero of an opera is quite as deserving of analytical study as the hero of a drama which is spoken. No labor would be lost in studying the character of Wagner's heroes in order to illuminate the impersonations of Niemann, Lehmann, or Scaria; nor is Maurel's *Iago* less worthy of investigation than Edwin Booth's.

The character of Delilah presents even more features of interest than that of the man of whom she was the undoing, and to those features I purpose to devote some attention presently.

There is no symbolism in Saint-Saëns's opera. It is frankly a piece for the lyric theatre, albeit one in which adherence to a plot suggested by the Biblical story compelled a paucity of action which had to be made good by spectacle and music. The best element in a drama being that which finds expression in action and dialogue, and these being restricted by the obvious desire of the composers to avoid such extraneous matter as Rossini and others were wont to use to add interest to their Biblical operas (the secondary love stories, for instance), Saint-Saëns could do nothing else than employ liberally the splendid factor of choral music which the oratorio form brought to his hand.

We are introduced to that factor without delay. Even before the first scene is opened to our eyes we hear the voice of the multitude in prayer. The *Israelites*, oppressed by their conquerors and sore stricken at the reflection that their God has deserted them, lament, accuse, protest, and pray. Before they have been heard, the poignancy of their woe has been published by the orchestra, which at once takes its place beside the chorus as a peculiarly eloquent expositor of the emotions and passions which propel the actors in the drama. That mission and that eloquence it maintains from the beginning to the final catastrophe, the instrumental band doing its share toward characterizing the opposing forces, emphasizing the solemn dignity of the Hebrew religion and contrasting it with the sensuous and sensual frivolity of the worshippers of Dagon. The choral prayer has for its instrumental substructure an obstinate syncopated figure,

which rises with the agonized cries of the people and sinks with their utterances of despair. The device of introducing voices before the disclosure of visible action in an opera is not new, and in this case is both uncalled for and ineffective. Gounod made a somewhat similar effort in his "Roméo et

Juliette," where a costumed group of singers presents
a prologue, vaguely visible through a gauze curtain.
Meyerbeer tried the expedient in "Le Pardon de
Ploërmel," and the siciliano in Mascagni's "Cavalleria rusticana" and the prologue in Leoncavallo's
"Pagliacci" are other cases in point. Of these
only the last can be said to achieve its purpose in
arresting the early attention of the audience. When
the curtain opens we see a public place in Gaza
in front of the temple of Dagon. The *Israelites*
are on their knees and in attitudes of mourning,
among them *Samson*. The voice of lamentation
takes a fugal form —

as the oppressed people tell of the sufferings which
they have endured : —

> Nous avons vu nos cités renversées
> Et les gentils profanants ton autel, etc.

The expression rises almost to the intensity of
sacrilegious accusation as the people recall to God
the vow made to them in Egypt, but sinks to accents
of awe when they reflect upon the incidents of their
former serfdom. Now *Samson* stands forth. In a
broad arioso, half recitative, half cantilena, wholly
in the oratorio style when it does not drop into the

mannerism of Meyerbeerian opera, he admonishes
his brethren of their need to trust in God, their duty
to worship Him, of His promises to aid them, of
the wonders that He had already wrought in their
behalf; he bids them to put off their doubts and
put on their armor of faith and valor. As he proceeds in his preachment he develops somewhat of
the theatrical pose of *John of Leyden* in "The
Prophet." The *Israelites* mutter gloomily of the
departure of their days of glory, but gradually take
warmth from the spirit which has obsessed *Samson*
and pledge themselves to do battle with the foe
with him under the guidance of Jehovah.

Now *Abimelech*, Satrap of Gaza, appears surrounded by Philistine soldiers. He rails at the
Israelites as slaves, sneers at their God as impotent
and craven, lifts up the horn of Dagon, who, he
says, shall pursue Jehovah as a falcon pursues a
dove. The speech fills *Samson* with a divine anger,
which bursts forth in a canticle of prayer and prophecy. There is a flash as of swords in the scintillant
scale passages which rush upward from the eager,
angry, pushing figure which mutters and rages
among the instruments. The *Israelites* catch fire
from *Samson's* ecstatic ardor and echo the words
in which he summons them to break their chains.
Abimelech rushes forward to kill *Samson*, but the
hero wrenches the sword from the Philistine's hand
and strikes him dead. The satrap's soldiers would
come to his aid, but are held in fear by the hero,

who is now armed. The *Israelites* rush off to make
war on their oppressors. The *High Priest* comes
down from the temple of Dagon and pauses where
the body of *Abimelech* lies. *Two Philistines* tell
of the fear which had paralyzed them when *Samson*
showed his might. The *High Priest* rebukes them
roundly for their cowardice, but has scarcely uttered
his denunciation before a *Messenger* enters to tell
him that *Samson* and his Israelitish soldiers have
overrun and ravaged the country. Curses and vows
of vengeance against Israel, her hero, and her God
from the mouth of Dagon's servant. One of his
imprecations is destined to be fulfilled : —

> Maudit soit le sein de la femme
> Qui lui donna le jour !
> Qu'enfin une compagne infame
> Trahisse son amour !

Revolutions run a rapid course in operatic Palestine. The insurrection is but begun with the slaying of *Abimelech*, yet as the *Philistines*, bearing away
his body, leave the scene, it is only to make room for
the *Israelites*, chanting of their victory. We expect
a sonorous hymn of triumph, but the people of God
have been chastened and awed by their quick deliverance, and their pæan is in the solemn tone of
temple psalmody, the first striking bit of local color
which the composer has introduced into his score —
a reticence on his part of which it may be said that it
is all the more remarkable from the fact that local
color is here completely justified : —

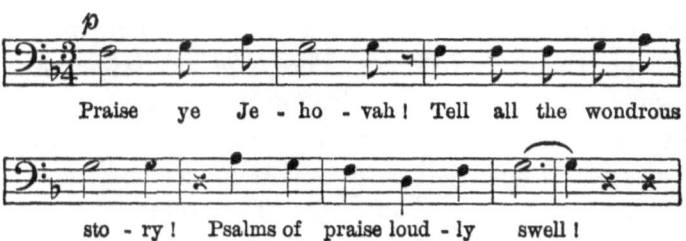

Praise ye Je - ho - vah! Tell all the wondrous sto - ry! Psalms of praise loud - ly swell!

> " Hymne de joie, hymne de délivrance
> Montez vers l'Eternel ! "

It is a fine piece of dramatic characterization, which is followed by one whose serene beauty is heightened by contrast. *Dalila* and a company of singing and dancing Philistine women come in bearing garlands of flowers. Not only *Samson's* senses, our own as well, are ravished by the delightful music : —

> Voici le printemps, nous portant des fleurs
> Pour orner le front des guerriers vainquers !
> Mêlons nos accents aux parfums des roses
>   A peine écloses !
> Avec l'oiseau chantons, mes sœurs !

Now Spring's generous hand, Brings flowers to the land.

Now Spring's generous hand, Brings flowers to the land.

Dalila is here and it is become necessary to say something of her, having said so much about the man whose destruction she accomplished. Let the ingenious and erudite Philip Hale introduce her: "Was Delilah a patriotic woman, to be ranked with Jael and Judith, or was she merely a courtesan, as certain opera singers who impersonate her in the opera seem to think? E. Meier says that the word 'Delilah' means 'the faithless one.' Ewald translates it 'traitress,' and so does Ranke. Knobel characterizes her as *die Zarte*, which means tender, delicate, but also subtle. Lange is sure that she was a weaver woman, if not an out-and-out 'zonah.' There are other Germans who think the word is akin to the verb *einlullen*, to lull asleep. Some liken it to the Arabic *dalilah*, a woman who misguides, a bawd. See in 'The Thousand Nights and a Night' the speech of the damsel to Aziz: 'If thou marry me thou wilt at least be safe from the daughter of Dalilah, the Wily One.' Also 'The Rogueries of Dalilah, the Crafty, and her daughter, Zayrah, the Coney Catcher.'"

We are directly concerned here with the *Dalila* of the opera, but Mr. Hale invites us to an excursion which offers a pleasant occupation for a brief while, and we cheerfully go with him. The Biblical Delilah is a vague figure, except in two respects: She is a woman of such charms that she wins the love of Samson, and such guile and cupidity that she plays upon his passion and betrays him to the

lords of the Philistines for pay. The Bible knows
nothing of her patriotism, nor does the sacred his-
torian give her the title of Samson's wife, though it
has long been the custom of Biblical commentators
to speak of her in this relation. St. Chrysostom
set the fashion and Milton followed it : —

> But who is this?   What thing of sea or land —
> Female of sex it seems —
> That, so bedeck'd, ornate and gay
> Comes this way sailing
> Like a stately ship
> Of Tarsus, bound for the isles
> Of Javan or Gadire,
> With all her bravery on, and tackle trim,
> Sails fill'd and streamers waving,
> Courted by all the winds that hold them play ;
> An amber scent of odorous perfume
> Her harbinger, a damsel train behind ?
> Some rich Philistian matron she may seem ;
> And now, at nearer view, no other certain
> Than Dalila, thy wife.

It cannot be without significance that the author
of the story in the Book of Judges speaks in a different way of each of the three women who play
a part in the tragedy of Samson's life.   The woman
who lived among the vineyards of Timnath, whose
murder Samson avenged, was his wife.   She was
a Philistine, but Samson married her according to
the conventional manner of the time and, also
according to the manner of the time, she kept her
home with her parents after her marriage.   Where-

fore she has gotten her name in the good books of
the sociological philosophers who uphold the mat-
ronymic theory touching early society. The woman
of Gaza whom Samson visited what time he confounded his would-be captors by carrying off the
doors of the gates of the city was curtly "an harlot."
Of the third woman it is said only that it came to
pass that Samson "loved a woman in the Valley
of Sorek, whose name was Delilah." Thereupon
follows the story of her bribery by the lords of the
Philistines and her betrayal of her lover. Evidently a licentious woman who could not aspire
even to the merit of the heroine of Dekker's play.

Milton not only accepted the theory of her wife-
hood, but also attributed patriotic motives to her.
She knew that her name would be defamed "in
Dan, in Judah and the bordering tribes."

> But in my country, where I most desire,
> In Eeron, Gaza, Asdod and in Gath,
> I shall be nam'd among the famousest
> Of women, sung at solemn festivals,
> Living and dead recorded, who to save
> Her country from a fierce destroyer, chose
> Above the faith of wedlock bands ; my tomb
> With odours visited and annual flowers ;
> Not less renown'd than in Mount Ephraim
> Jael, who, with inhospitable guile,
> Smote Sisera sleeping.

In the scene before us *Dalila* is wholly and simply
a siren, a seductress who plays upon the known love

of *Samson* from motives which are not disclosed.
As yet one may imagine her moved by a genuine
passion. She turns her lustrous black eyes upon
him as she hails him a double victor over his foes
and her heart, and invites him to rest from his arms
in her embraces in the fair valley of Sorek. Temptation seizes upon the soul of *Samson*. He prays
God to make him steadfast; but she winds her toils
the tighter: It is for him that she has bound a
coronet of purple grapes upon her forehead and
entwined the rose of Sharon in her ebon tresses.
An Old Hebrew warns against the temptress and
Samson agonizingly invokes a veil over the beauty
that has enchained him.

"Extinguish the fires of those eyes which enslave
me." — thus he.

"Sweet is the lily of the valley, pleasant the
juices of mandragora, but sweeter and more pleasant
are my kisses!" — thus she.

The *Old Hebrew* warns again: "If thou give ear
to her honeyed phrases, my son, curses will alight
on thee which no tears that thou may'st weep
will ever efface."

But still the siren song rings in his ears. The
maidens who had come upon the scene with *Dalila*
(are they priestesses of Dagon?) dance, swinging
their floral garlands seductively before the eyes of
Samson and his followers. The hero tries to avoid
the glances which *Dalila*, joining in the dance,
throws upon him. It is in vain; his eyes follow

her through all the voluptuous postures and movements of the dance.

And *Dalila* sings "Printemps qui commence" — a song often heard in concert-rooms, but not so often as the air with which the love-duet in the second act reaches its culmination, which is popularly held also to mark the climax of the opera. That song is wondrously insinuating in its charm; it pulsates with passion, so much so, indeed, that it is difficult to conceive that its sentiments are feigned, but this is lovelier in its fresh, suave, graceful, and healthy beauty : —

The Spring with her dow - er of bird and of flow - er, brings hope in her train.

As *Dalila* leaves the scene her voice and eyes
repeat their lure, while *Samson's* looks and acts
betray the trouble of his soul.

It is not until we see and hear *Dalila* in the second
act that she is revealed to us in her true character.
Not till now does she disclose the motives of her
conduct toward her lover.   Night is falling in the
valley of Sorek, the vale which lies between the hill
country which the Israelites entered from the East,
and the coast land which the Philistines, supposedly
an island people, invaded from the West.   *Dalila,*
gorgeously apparelled, is sitting on a rock near the
portico of her house.   The strings of the orchestra
murmur and the chromatic figure which we shall
hear again in her love-song coos in the wood-winds:

She awaits him whom passion has made her
slave in full confidence of her hold upon him.

Samson, recherchant ma présence,
Ce soir doit venir en ces lieux.
Voici l'heure de la vengeance
Qui doit satisfaire nos dieux !

Amour ! viens aider ma faiblesse !

The vengeance of her gods shall be glutted; it
is to that end she invokes the power of love to
strengthen her weakness. A passion like his will
not down — that she knows. To her comes the
High Priest: Samson's strength, he says, is super-
natural and flows from a vow with which he was
consecrated to effect the glory of Israel. Once while
he lay in her arms that strength had deserted him,
but now, it is said, he flouts her love and doubts his
own passion. There is no need to try to awaken

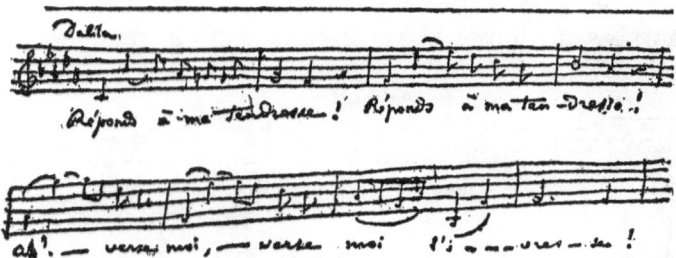

jealousy in the heart of *Dalila;* she hates *Samson*
more bitterly than the leader of his enemies. She
is not mercenary, like the Biblical woman; she
scorns the promise of riches which the *High Priest*
offers so she obtain the secret of the Hebrew's
strength. Thrice had she essayed to learn that
secret and thrice had he set her spell at naught.
Now she will assail him with tears — a woman's
weapon.

The rumblings of thunder are heard; the scene is
lit up by flashes of lightning. Running before

the storm, which is only a precursor and a symbol
of the tempest which is soon to rend his soul, *Samson* comes. *Dalila* upbraids her lover, rebukes his
fears, protests her grief. *Samson* cannot with-
stand her tears. He confesses his love, but he
must obey the will of a higher power. "What god
is mightier than Love?" Let him but doubt
her constancy and she will die. And she plays her
trump card: "Mon cœur s'ouvre à ta voix," while
the fluttering strings and cooing wood-winds insinu-
ate themselves into the crevices of *Samson's* moral
harness and loosen the rivets that hold it together : —

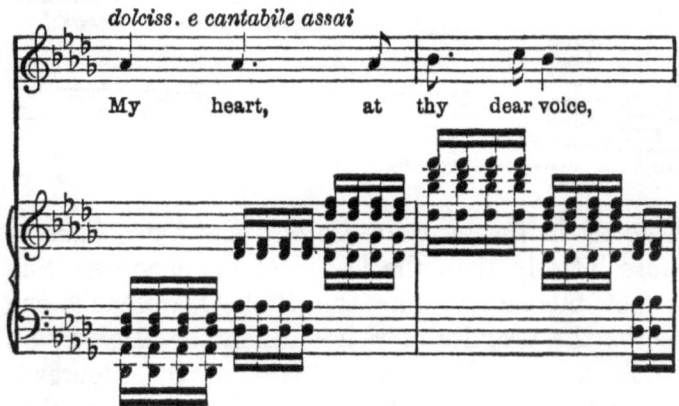

Herein lies the strength and the weakness of
music: it must fain be truthful. *Dalila's* words
may be hypocritical, but the music speaks the
speech of genuine passion. Not until we hear
the refrain echoed mockingly in the last scene of

the drama can we believe that the passion hymned
in this song is feigned. And we almost deplore
that the composer put it to such disgraceful use.
Samson hears the voice of his God in the growing
storm and again hesitates. The storm bursts
as *Dalila* shrieks out the hate that fills her and runs
toward her dwelling.

Beethoven sought to suggest external as well
as internal peace in the "Dona nobis" of his Mass
in D by mingling the sounds of war with the prayer
for peace; Saint-Saëns pictures the storm in nature
and in *Samson's* soul by the music which accompanies the hero as he raises his hands mutely in
prayer; then follows the temptress with faltering
steps and enters her dwelling. The tempest reaches
its climax; *Dalila* appears at the window with a
shout to the waiting Philistine soldiery below. The
voice of *Samson* cuts through the stormy night:
"Trahison !"

Act III. — First scene: A prison in Gaza. *Samson*, shorn of his flowing locks, which as a Nazarite
he had vowed should never be touched by shears,
labors at the mill. He has been robbed of his
eyes and darkness has settled down upon him; darkness, too, upon the people whom his momentary
weakness had given back into slavery.

"Total eclipse !" Saint-Saëns has won our admiration for the solemn dignity with which he has
invested the penitent confession of the blind hero.
But who shall hymn the blindness of Manoah's

son after Milton and Handel? From a crowd of captive *Hebrews* outside the prison walls come taunting accusations, mingled with supplications to God. We recognize again the national mood of the psalmody of the first act. The entire scene is finely conceived. It is dramatic in a lofty sense, for its action plays on the stage of the heart. *Samson*, contrite, humble, broken in spirit, with a prayer for his people's deliverance, is led away to be made sport of in the temple of Dagon. There, before the statue of the god, grouped among the columns and before the altar the *High Priest* and the lords of the Philistines. *Dalila*, too, with maidens clad for the lascivious dance, and the multitude of Philistia. The women's choral song to spring which charmed us in the first act is echoed by mixed voices. The ballet which follows is a prettily exotic one, with an introductory cadence marked by the Oriental scale, out of which the second dance melody is constructed — a scale which has the peculiarity of an interval composed of three semitones, and which we know from the song of the priestesses in Verdi's " Aïda " : —

The *High Priest* makes mock of the Judge of Israel: Let him empty the wine cup and sing the praise of his vanquisher! *Dalila*, in the pride of her triumph, tauntingly tells him how simulated love had been made to serve her gods, her hate, and her nation. *Samson* answers only in contrite prayer. Together in canonic imitation (the erudite form does not offend, but only gives dignity to the scene) priest and siren offer a libation on the altar of the Fish god.

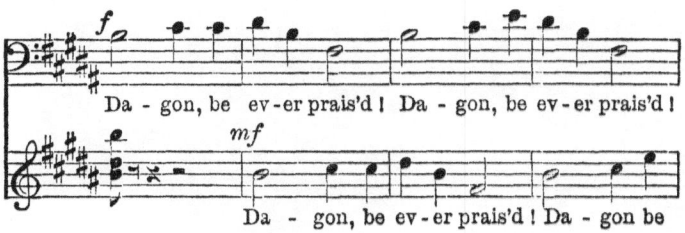

The flames flash upward from the altar. Now a supreme act of insolent impiety; *Samson*, too, shall sacrifice to Dagon. A boy is told to lead him where all can witness his humiliation. *Samson* feels that the time for retribution upon his enemies

is come. He asks to be led between the marble
pillars that support the roof of the temple. Priests
and people, the traitress and her dancing women,
the lords of the Philistines, the rout of banqueters
and worshippers — all hymn the praise of Dagon.
A brief supplication to Israel's God —

"And Samson took hold.of the two middle pillars
upon which the house stood and on which it was borne
up, of the one with his right hand and of the other with
his left.

"And Samson said, 'Let me die with the Philistines.'
And he bowed himself with all his might : and the house
fell upon the lords and upon all the people that were
therein. So the dead which he slew at his death were
more than they which he slew in his life."

CHAPTER V

THE most obvious reason why Goldmark's "Königin von Saba" should be seen and heard with pleasure lies in its book and scenic investiture. Thoughtfully considered the book is not one of great worth, but in the handling of things which give pleasure to the superficial observer it is admirable. In the first place it presents a dramatic story which is rational; which strongly enlists the interest if not the sympathies of the observer; which is unhackneyed; which abounds with imposing spectacles with which the imagination of childhood already had made play, that are not only intrinsically brilliant and fascinating but occur as necessary adjuncts of the story. Viewed from its ethical side and considered with reference to the sources whence its elements sprang, it falls under a considerable measure of condemnation, as will more plainly appear after its incidents have been rehearsed.

The title of the opera indicates that the Biblical story of the visit of the Queen of Sheba to Solomon had been drawn on for the plot. This is true, but only in a slight degree. *Sheba's Queen* comes to

G 81

Solomon in the opera, but that is the end of the draft on the Scriptural legend so far as she is concerned. *Sulamith*, who figures in the drama, owes her name to the Canticles, from which it was borrowed by the librettist, but no element of her character nor any of the incidents in which she is involved. The "Song of Songs, which is Solomon's" contributes a few lines of poetry to the book, and a ritualistic service which is celebrated in the temple finds its original text in the opening verses of Psalms lxvii and cxvii, but with this I have enumerated all that the opera owes to the Bible. It is not a Biblical opera, in the degree that Méhul's "Joseph," Rossini's "Moses," or Rubinstein's "Maccabees" is Biblical, to say nothing of Saint-Saëns's "Samson et Dalila." Solomon's magnificent reign and marvellous wisdom, which contribute a few factors to the sum of the production, belong to profane as well as to sacred history and it will be found most agreeable to deeply rooted preconceptions to think of some other than the Scriptural Solomon as the prototype of the *Solomon* of Mosenthal and Goldmark, who, at the best, is a sorry sort of sentimentalist. The local color has been borrowed from the old story; the dramatic motive comes plainly from Wagner's "Tannhäuser."

Assad, a favorite courtier, is sent by *Solomon* to extend greetings and a welcome to the *Queen of Sheba*, who is on the way to visit the king, whose fame for wealth and wisdom has reached her ears in far Arabia.   *Assad* is the type (though a milk-and-watery one, it must be confessed) of manhood struggling between the things that are of the earth and the things which are of heaven — between a gross, sensual passion and a pure, exalting love.   He is betrothed to *Sulamith*, the daughter of the *High Priest* of the temple, who awaits his return from *Solomon's* palace and leads her companions in songs of gladness.   *Assad* meets the *Queen* at Gath, performs his mission, and sets out to return, but, exhausted by the heat of the day, enters the forest on Mount Lebanon and lies down on a bank of moss to rest.   There the sound of plashing waters arrests his ear.   He seeks the cause of the grateful noise and comes upon a transportingly beautiful woman bathing.   The nymph, finding herself observed, does not, like another Diana, cause the death of her admirer, but discloses herself to be a veritable Wagnerian *Venus*.   She clips him in her arms and he falls at her feet ; but a reed rustles and the charmer flees.   These incidents we do not see.   They precede the opening of the opera, and we learn of them from *Assad's* narration.   *Assad* returns to Jerusalem, where, conscience stricken, he seeks to avoid his chaste bride.   To *Solomon*, however, he confesses his adventure, and the king sets the morrow as his wedding day with *Sulamith*.

The *Queen of Sheba* arrives, and when she raises her veil, ostensibly to show unto *Solomon* the first view of her features that mortal man has ever had

vouchsafed him, *Assad* recognizes the heroine of his
adventure in the woods on Lebanon. His mind
is in a maze; bewilderingly he addresses her, and
haughtily he is repulsed. But the woman has felt
the dart no less than *Assad;* she seeks him at night
in the palace garden, whither she had gone to brood
over her love and the loss which threatens her on the
morrow, and the luring song of her slave draws him
again into her arms.

Before the altar in the temple, just as *Assad* is
about to pronounce the words which are to bind him
to *Sulamith,* she confronts him again, on the specious
pretext that she brings gifts for the bride. *Assad*
again addresses her. Again he is denied. Delirium
seizes upon his brain; he loudly proclaims the *Queen*
as the goddess of his devotion. The people are
panic-stricken at the sacrilege and rush from the
temple; the priests cry anathema; *Sulamith* bemoans her fate; *Solomon* essays words of comfort;
the *High Priest* intercedes with heaven; the soldiery,
led by *Baal-Hanan,* overseer of the palace, enter
to lead the profaner to death. Now *Solomon* claims
the right to fix his punishment. The *Queen,* fearful
that her prey may escape her, begs his life as a boon,
but *Solomon* rejects her appeal; *Assad* must work out
his salvation by overcoming temptation and master-
ing his wicked passion. *Sulamith* approaches amid
the wailings of her companions. She is about to enter
a retreat on the edge of the Syrian desert, but she,
too, prays for the life of *Assad. Solomon,* in a

prophetic ecstasy, foretells *Assad's* deliverance from sin and in a vision sees a meeting between him and his pure love under a palm tree in the desert. *Assad* is banished to the sandy waste; there a simoom sweeps down upon him; he falls at the foot of a lonely palm to die, after calling on *Sulamith* with his fleeting breath. She comes with her wailing maidens, sees the fulfilment of *Solomon's* prophecy, and *Assad* dies in her arms. "Thy beloved is thine, in love's eternal realm," sing the maidens, while a mirage shows the wicked *Queen*, with her caravan of camels and elephants, returning to her home.

The parallel between this story and the immeasurably more poetical and beautiful one of "Tannhäuser" is apparent to half an eye. *Sulamith* is *Elizabeth*, the *Queen* is *Venus*, *Assad* is *Tannhäuser*, *Solomon* is *Wolfram von Eschenbach*. The ethical force of the drama — it has some, though very little — was weakened at the performances at the Metropolitan Opera House [1] in New York by the excision

---

[1] Goldmark's opera was presented for the first time in America at the Metropolitan Opera House on December 2, 1885. Cast: *Sulamith*, Fräulein Lilli Lehmann; *die Königin von Saba*, Frau Krämer-Wiedl; *Astaroth*, Fräulein Marianne Brandt; *Solomon*, Herr Adolph Robinson; *Assad*, Herr Stritt; *Der Hohe Priester*, Herr Emil Fischer; *Baal-Hanan*, Herr-Alexi. Anton Seidl conducted, and the opera had fifteen representations in the season. These performances were in the original German. On April 3, 1888, an English version was presented at the Academy of Music by the National Opera Company, then in its death throes. The opera was revived at the Metropolitan Opera House by Mr. Conried in the season 1905–1906 and had five performances.

from the last act of a scene in which the *Queen*
attempts to persuade *Assad* to go with her to Arabia.
Now *Assad* rises superior to his grosser nature and
drives the temptress away, thus performing the
saving act demanded by *Solomon*.

Herr Mosenthal, who made the libretto of "Die
Königin von Saba," treated this material, not with
great poetic skill, but with a cunning appreciation of
the opportunities which it offers for dramatic effect.
The opera opens with a gorgeous picture of the
interior of *Solomon's* palace, decked in honor of the
coming guest.   There is an air of joyous expectancy
over everything. *Sulamith's* entrance introduces
the element of female charm to brighten the brilliancy of the picture, and her bridal song — in which
the refrain is an excerpt from the Canticles, "Thy
beloved is thine, who feeds among the roses" —
enables the composer to indulge his strong predilection and fecund gift for Oriental melody.   The
action hurries to a thrilling climax.   One glittering
pageant treads on the heels of another, each more
gorgeous and resplendent than the last, until the
stage, set to represent a fantastical hall with a be-
wildering vista of carved columns, golden lions, and
rich draperies, is filled with such a kaleidoscopic mass
of colors and groupings as only an Oriental mind
could conceive.   Finally all the preceding strokes
are eclipsed by the coming of the *Queen*.   But no
time is lost ; the spectacle does not make the action
halt for a moment. *Sheba* makes her gifts and

uncovers her face, and at once we are confronted by the tragical element, and the action rushes on toward its legitimate and mournful end.

In this ingenious blending of play and spectacle one rare opportunity after another is presented to the composer. *Sulamith's* epithalamium, *Assad's* narrative, the choral greeting to the *Queen*, the fateful recognition — all these things are made for music of the inspiring, swelling, passionate kind. In the second act, the *Queen's* monologue, her duet with *Assad*, and, most striking of all, the unaccompanied bit of singing with which *Astaroth* lures *Assad* into the presence of the *Queen*, who is hiding in the shadow of broad-leaved palms behind a running fountain — a melodic phrase saturated with the mystical color of the East — these are gifts of the rarest kind to the composer, which he has enriched to give them in turn to the public. That relief from their stress of passion is necessary is not forgotten, but is provided in the ballet music and the solemn ceremonial in the temple, which takes place amid surroundings that call into active operation one's childhood fancies touching the sacred fane on Mount Moriah and the pompous liturgical functions of which it was the theatre.

Goldmark's music is highly spiced. He was an eclectic, and his first aim seems to have been to give the drama a tonal investiture which should be in keeping with its character, external as well as internal. At times his music rushes along like a lava stream of passion, every measure pulsating with eager, excited, and exciting life. He revels in instrumental color. The language of his orchestra is as glowing as the poetry attributed to the royal poet whom his operatic story celebrates. Many composers before him made use of Oriental cadences, rhythms, and idioms, but to none do they seem to have come so like native language as to Goldmark. It is romantic music, against which the strongest objection that can be urged is that it is so unvaryingly stimulated that it wearies the mind and makes the listener long for a change to a fresher and healthier musical atmosphere.

CHAPTER VI

"HÉRODIADE"

In the ballet scene of Gounod's most popular opera *Mephistopheles* conjures up visions of Phryne, Laïs, Aspasia, Cleopatra, and Helen of Troy to beguile the jaded interest of *Faust*. The list reads almost like a catalogue of the operas of Massenet whose fine talent was largely given to the celebration of the famous courtesans of the ancient world. With the addition of a few more names from the roster of antiquity (*Thaïs, Dalila,* and *Aphrodite*), and some less ancient but no less immoral creatures of modern fancy, like *Violetta, Manon Lescaut, Zaza,* and *Louise,* we might make a pretty complete list of representatives of the female type in which modern dramatists and composers seem to think the interest of humanity centres.

When Massenet's "Hérodiade" was announced as the first opera to be given at the Manhattan Opera House in New York for the season of 1909–1910 it looked to some observers as if the dominant note of the year was to be sounded by the Scarlet Woman; but the representation brought a revelation and a surprise. The names of the principal characters

89

were those which for a few years had been filling
the lyric theatres of Germany with a moral stench;
but their bearers in Massenet's opera did little or
nothing that was especially shocking to good taste
or proper morals. *Herod* was a love-sick man of
lust, who gazed with longing eyes upon the physical
charms of *Salomé* and pleaded for her smiles like any
sentimental milksop; but he did not offer her
Capernaum for a dance. *Salomé* may have known
how, but she did not dance for either half a kingdom
or the whole of a man's head. Instead, though
there were intimations that her reputation was not
all that a good maiden's ought to be, she sang pious
hosannahs and waved a palm branch conspicuously
in honor of the prophet at whose head she had
bowled herself in the desert, the public streets, and
king's palaces. At the end she killed herself when
she found that the vengeful passion of *Herodias* and
the jealous hatred of *Herod* had compassed the death
of the saintly man whom she had loved. *Herodias*
was a wicked woman, no doubt, for *John the Baptist*
denounced her publicly as a Jezebel, but her jealousy
of *Salomé* had reached a point beyond her control
before she learned that her rival was her own daughter whom she had deserted for love of the Tetrarch.
As for *John the Baptist* the camel's hair with which
he was clothed must have cost as pretty a penny as
any of the modern kind, and if he wore a girdle of
skins about his loins it was concealed under a really
regal cloak. He was a voice; but not one crying

in the wilderness. He was in fact an operatic tenor *comme il faut*, who needed only to be shut up in a subterranean jail with the young woman who had pursued him up hill and down dale, in and out of season to make love to her in the most approved fashion of the Paris Grand Opéra.

What shall we think of the morals of this French opera, after we have seen and heard that compounded by the Englishman Oscar Wilde and the German Richard Strauss? No wonder that England's Lord Chamberlain asked nothing more than an elimination of the Biblical names when he licensed a performance of "Hérodiade" at Covent Garden. There was no loss of dramatic qualitiy in calling *Herod, Moriame*, and *Herodias, Hesotade*, and changing the scene from Jerusalem to Azoum in Ethiopia; though it must have been a trifle diverting to hear fair-skinned Ethiopians singing *Schma Yisroel, Adonai Elohenu* in a temple which could only be that of Jerusalem. John the Baptist was only *Jean* in the original and needed not to be changed, and *Salomé* is not in the Bible, though Salome, a very different woman is — a fact which the Lord Chamberlain seems to have overlooked when he changed the title of the opera from "Hérodiade" to "Salomé."

Where does Salome come from, anyway? And where did she get her chameleonlike nature? Was she an innocent child, as Flaubert represents her, who could but lisp the name of the prophet when her mother told her to ask for his head? Had she

taken dancing lessons from one of the women of
Cadiz to learn to dance as she must have danced to
excite such lust in Herod? Was she a monster, a
worse than vampire as she is represented by Wilde
and Strauss? Was she an "Israelitish grisette" as
Pougin called the heroine of the opera which it
took one Italian (Zanardini) and three Frenchmen
(Milliet, Grémont, and Massenet) to concoct? No
wonder that the brain of Saint-Saëns reeled when he
went to hear "Hérodiade" at its first performance
in Brussels and found that the woman whom he had
looked upon as a type of lasciviousness and mon-
strous cruelty had become metamorphosed into a
penitent Magdalen. Read the plot of the opera and
wonder !

Salomé is a maiden in search of her mother whom
John the Baptist finds in his wanderings and be-
friends. She clings to him when he becomes a political as well as a religious power among the Jews,
though he preaches unctuously to her touching the
vanity of earthly love. *Herodias* demands his
death of her husband for that he had publicly in-
sulted her, but *Herod* schemes to use his influence
over the Jews to further his plan to become a real
monarch instead of a Roman Tetrarch. But when
the pro-consul *Vitellius* wins the support of the
people and *Herod* learns that the maiden who has
spurned him is in love with the prophet, he decrees
his decapitation. *Salomé*, baffled in her effort to
save her lover, attempts to kill *Herodias;* but the

wicked woman discloses herself as the maiden's mother and *Salomé* turns the dagger against her own breast.

This is all of the story one needs to know. It is richly garnished with incident, made gorgeous with pageantry, and clothed with much charming music. Melodies which may be echoes of synagogal hymns of great antiquity resound in the walls of the temple at Jerusalem, in which respect the opera recalls Goldmark's "Queen of Sheba." Curved Roman trumpets mix their loud clangors with the instruments of the modern brass band and compel us to think of "Aïda." There are dances of Egyptians, Babylonians, and Phœnicians, and if the movements of the women make us deplore the decay of the choreographic art, the music warms us almost as much as the Spanish measures in "Le Cid." Eyes and ears are deluged with Oriental color until at the last there comes a longing for the graciously insinuating sentimentalities of which the earlier Massenet was a master. Two of the opera's airs had long been familiar to the public from performance in the concert-room — *Salomé's* "Il est doux" and *Herod's* "Vision fugitive" — and they stand out as the brightest jewels in the opera's musical crown; but there is much else which woos the ear delightfully, for Massenet was ever a gracious if not a profound melodist and a master of construction and theatrical orchestration. When he strives for massive effects, however, he sometimes becomes futile, banal where he would be imposing; but he commands a charm which is insinuating in its moments of intimacy.[1]

[1] "Hérodiade" had its first performance in New York (it had previously been given in New Orleans by the French Opera Company) on November 8, 1909. The cast was as follows: *Salomé*, Lina Cavalieri; *Herodias*, Gerville-Reache; *John*, Charles Dalmores; *Herod*, Maurice Renaud; *Vitellius*, Crabbé; *Phanuel*, M. Vallier; *High Priest*, M. Nicolay. Musical director, Henriques de la Fuente.

CHAPTER VII

"LAKMÉ"

Lakmé is the daughter of *Nilakantha*, a fanatical
Brahmin priest, who has withdrawn to a ruined
temple deep in an Indian forest. In his retreat the
old man nurses his wrath against the British invader,
prays assiduously to Brahma (thus contributing a
fascinating Oriental mood to the opening of the
opera), and waits for the time to come when he shall
be able to wreak his revenge on the despoilers of his
country. *Lakmé* sings Oriental duets with her slave,
Mallika:—

> Sous le dôme épais où le blanc jasmin
> A la rose s'assemble,
> Sur la rive en fleurs, riant au matin
> Viens, descendons ensemble —

a dreamy, sense-ensnaring, hypnotic barcarole. The
opera opens well; by this time the composer has
carried us deep into the jungle. The Occident is
rude: *Gerald*, an English officer, breaks through a
bamboo fence and makes love to *Lakmé*, who, though
widely separated from her operatic colleagues from
an ethnological point of view like *Elsa* and *Senta*,

95

to expedite the action requites the passion instanter. After the Englishman is gone the father returns and, with an Oriental's cunning which does him credit, deduces from the broken fence that an Englishman has profaned the sacred spot. This is the business of Act I. In Act II the father, disguised as a beggar who holds a dagger ever in readiness, and his daughter, disguised as a street singer, visit a town market in search of the profaner. The business is not to *Lakmé's* taste, but it is not for the like of her to neglect the opportunity offered to win applause with the legend of the pariah's daughter, with its tintinnabulatory charm : —

> Ou va la jeune Hindoue
> Fille des parias;
> Quand la lune se joue
> Dans les grand mimosas?

It is the "Bell song," which has tinkled so often in our concert-rooms. *Gerald* recognizes the singer despite her disguise; and *Nilakantha* recognizes him as the despoiler of the hallowed spot in which he worships and incidentally conceals his daughter. The bloodthirsty fanatic observes sententiously that Brahma has smiled and cuts short *Gerald's* soliloquizing with a dagger thrust. *Lakmé*, with the help of a male slave, removes him to a hut concealed in the forest. While he is convalescing the pair sing duets and exchange vows of undying affection. But the military Briton, who has invaded the country at large, must needs now invade also this cosey abode of love. *Frederick*, a brother officer, discovers *Gerald* and informs him that duty calls (Britain always expects every man to do his duty, no matter what the consequences to him) and he must march with his regiment. *Frederick* has happened in just as *Lakmé* is gone for some sacred water in which she and *Gerald* were to pledge eternal love for each other, to each other. But, spurred on by *Frederick* and the memory that "England expects, etc.," *Gerald* finds the call of the fife and drum more potent than the voice of love. *Lakmé*, psychologist as well as botanist, understands the struggle which now takes place in *Gerald's* soul, and relieves him of his dilemma by crushing a poisonous flower (to be exact, the *Datura stramonium*) between her teeth, dying, it would seem, to the pious delight of her father, who "ecstatically" beholds her dwelling with Brahma.

The story, borrowed by Gondinet and Gille from the little romance "Le Mariage de Loti," is worthless except to furnish motives for tropical scenery, Hindu dresses, and Oriental music. Three English ladies, *Ellen*, *Rose*, and *Mrs. Bentson*, figure in the play, but without dramatic purpose except to take part in some concerted music. They are, indeed, so insignificant in all other respects that when the opera was given by Miss Van Zandt and a French company in London for the first time in 1885 they were omitted, and the excision was commended by the critics, who knew that it had been made. The conversation of the women is all of the veriest stopgap

H

character. The maidens, *Rose* and *Ellen,* are English ladies visiting in the East; *Mrs. Bentson* is their chaperon. All that they have to say is highly unimportant, even when true. "What do you see, *Frederick?*" "A garden." "And you, *Gerald?*" "Big, beautiful trees." "Anybody about?" "Don't know." "Look again." "That's not easy; the fence shuts out the view within." "Can't you make a peephole through the bamboo?" "Girls, girls, be careful." And so on and so on for quantity. But we must fill three acts, and ensemble makes its demands; besides, we want pretty blondes of the English type to put in contrast with the dark-skinned *Lakmé* and her slave. At the first representation in New York by the American Opera Company, at the Academy of Music, on March 1, 1886, the three women were permitted to interfere with what there is of poetical spirit in the play, and their conversation, like that of the other principals, was uttered in the recitatives composed by Delibes to take the place of the spoken dialogue used at the Paris Opéra Comique, where spoken dialogue is traditional. Theodore Thomas conducted the Academy performance, at which the cast was as follows: *Lakmé*, Pauline L'Allemand; *Nilakantha*, Alonzo E. Stoddard; *Gerald*, William Candidus; *Frederick*, William H. Lee; *Ellen*, Charlotte Walker; *Rose*, Helen Dudley Campbell; *Mrs. Bentson*, May Fielding; *Mallika*, Jessie Bartlett Davis; *Hadji*, William H. Fessenden.

Few operas have had a more variegated American

history than "Lakmé." It was quite new when it was first heard in New York, but it had already given rise to considerable theatrical gossip, not to say scandal. The first representation took place at the Opéra Comique in April, 1883, with Miss Marie Van Zandt, an American girl, the daughter of a singer who had been actively successful in English opera in New York and London, as creator of the part of the heroine. The opera won a pretty triumph and so did the singer. At once there was talk of a New York performance. Mme. Etelka Gerster studied the titular rôle with M. Delibes and, as a member of Colonel Mapleson's company at the Academy of Music, confidently expected to produce the work there in the season of 1883–1884, the first season of the rivalry between the Academy and the Metropolitan Opera House, which had just opened its doors; but though she went so far as to offer to buy the American performing rights from Heugel, the publisher, nothing came of it. The reason was easily guessed by those who knew that there has been, or was pending, a quarrel between Colonel Mapleson and M. Heugel concerning the unauthorized use by the impresario of other scores owned by the publisher.

During the same season, however, Miss Emma Abbott carried a version (or rather a perversion) of the opera, for which the orchestral parts had been arranged from the pianoforte score, into the cities of the West, and brought down a deal of unmerited criticism on the innocent head of M. Delibes. In

the season of 1884–1885 Colonel Mapleson came back
to the Academy with vouchers of various sorts to
back up a promise to give the opera.   There was a
human voucher in the person of Miss Emma Nevada,
who had also enjoyed the instruction of the composer
and who had trunkfuls and trunkfuls and trunkfuls
of Oriental dresses, though *Lakmé* needs but few.
There were gorgeous uniforms for the British soldiers,
the real article, each scarlet coat and every top boot
having a piece of history attached, and models of the
scenery which any doubting Thomas of a newspaper
reporter might inspect if he felt so disposed.   When
the redoubtable colonel came it was to be only a
matter of a week or so before the opera would be put
on the stage in the finest of styles; it was still a
matter of a week or so when the Academy season
came to an end.   When Delibes's exquisite and exotic
music reached a hearing in the American metropolis,
it was sung to English words, and the most emphatic
success achieved in performance was the acrobatic
one of Mme. L'Allemand as she rolled down some
uncalled-for pagoda steps in the death scene.

Mme. Adelina Patti was the second *Lakmé* heard
in New York.   After the fifth season of German
opera at the Metropolitan Opera House had come to
an end in the spring of 1890, Messrs. Abbey and Grau
took the theatre for a short season of Italian opera
by a troupe headed by Mme. Patti.   In that season
"Lakmé" was sung once — on April 2, 1890.   Now
came an opportunity for the original representative

of the heroine. Abbey and Grau resumed the management of the theatre in 1891, and in their company was Miss Van Zandt, for whom the opera was "revived" on February 22. Mr. Abbey had great expectations, but they were disappointed. For the public there was metal more attractive than Miss Van Zandt and the Hindu opera in other members of the company and other operas. It was the year of Emma Eames's coming and also of Jean de Reszke's (they sang together in Gounod's "Roméo et Juliette") and "Cavalleria rusticana" was new. Then Delibes's opera hibernated in New York for fifteen years, after which the presence in the Metropolitan company of Mme. Marcella Sembrich led to another "revival." (Operas which are unperformed for a term of two or three years after having been once included in the repertory are "revived" in New York.) It was sung three times in the season of 1906–1907. It also afforded one of Mr. Hammerstein's many surprises at the Manhattan Opera House. Five days before the close of his last season, on March 21, 1910, it was precipitated on the stage ("pitchforked" is the popular and professional term) to give Mme. Tetrazzini a chance to sing the bell song. Altogether I know of no more singular history than that of "Lakmé" in New York.

Lakmé is a child of the theatrical boards, who inherited traits from several predecessors, the strong-

est being those deriving from *Aïda* and *Selika*.   Like
the former, she loves a man whom her father believes
to be the arch enemy of his native land, and, like her,
she is the means of betraying him into the hands of
the avenger.   Like the heroine of Meyerbeer's post-
humous opera, she has a fatal acquaintance with
tropical botany and uses her knowledge to her own
destruction.   Her scientific attainments are on about
the same plane as her amiability, her abnormal
sense of filial duty, and her musical accomplishments.
She loves a man whom her father wishes her to lure
to his death by her singing, and she sings entrancingly
enough to bring about the meeting between her
lover's back and her father's knife.   That she does
not warble herself into the position of *particeps
criminis* in a murder she owes only to the bungling
of the old man.   Having done this, however, she
turns physician and nurse and brings the wounded
man back to health, thus sacrificing her love to the
duty which her lover thinks he owes to the invaders
of her country and oppressors of her people.   After
this she makes the fatal application of her botanical
knowledge.   Such things come about when one goes
to India for an operatic heroine.

The feature of the libretto which Delibes has used
to the best purpose is its local color.   His music is
saturated with the languorous spirit of the East.
Half a dozen of the melodies are lovely inventions,
of marked originality in both matter and treatment,
and the first half hour of the opera is apt to take one's

fancy completely captive. The drawback lies in the oppressive weariness which succeeds the first trance, and is brought on by the monotonous character of the music. After an hour of "Lakmé" one yearns for a few crashing chords of C major as a person enduring suffocation longs for a gush of fresh air. The music first grows monotonous, then wearies. Delibes's lyrical moments show the most numerous indications of beauty; dramatic life and energy are absent from the score. In the second act he moves his listeners only once — with the attempted repetition of the bell song after *Lakmé* has recognized her lover. The odor of the poppy invites to drowsy enjoyment in the beginning, and the first act is far and away the most gratifying in the opera, musically as well as scenically. It would be so if it contained only *Lakmé's* song "Pourquoi dans les grands bois," the exquisite barcarole — a veritable treasure trove for the composer, who used its melody dramatically throughout the work — and *Gerald's* air, "Fantaisie aux divins mensonges." Real depth will be looked for in vain in this opera; superficial loveliness is apparent on at least half its pages.

CHAPTER VIII

"PAGLIACCI"

FOR a quarter of a century "Cavalleria rusticana"
and "Pagliacci" have been the Castor and Pollux
of the operatic theatres of Europe and America.
Together they have joined the hunt of venturesome
impresarios for that Calydonian boar, success;
together they have lighted the way through seasons
of tempestuous stress and storm. Of recent years
at the Metropolitan Opera House in New York
efforts have been made to divorce them and to find
associates for one or the other, since neither is sufficient in time for an evening's entertainment; but
they refuse to be put asunder as steadfastly as did
the twin brothers of Helen and Clytemnestra. There
has been no operatic Zeus powerful enough to separate and alternate their existences even for a day;
and though blasé critics will continue to rail at the
"double bill" as they have done for two decades or
more, the two fierce little dramas will "sit shining
on the sails" of many a managerial ship and bring
it safe to haven for many a year to come.

Twins the operas are in spirit; twins in their
capacity as supreme representatives of *verismo*;

twins in the fitness of their association; but twins
they are not in respect of parentage or age. "Cavalleria rusticana" is two years older than "Pagliacci"
and as truly its progenitor as Weber's operas were the
progenitors of Wagner's. They are the offspring of
the same artistic movement, and it was the phe-

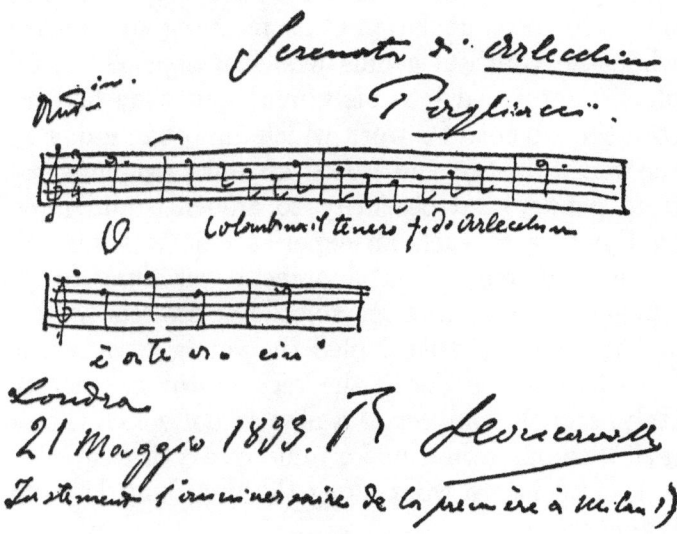

nomenal success of Mascagni's opera which was the
spur that drove Leoncavallo to write his. When
"Cavalleria rusticana" appeared on the scene, two
generations of opera-goers had passed away without
experiencing anything like the sensation caused
by this opera. They had witnessed the production,
indeed, of great masterpieces, which it would be

almost sacrilegious to mention in the same breath
with Mascagni's turbulent and torrential tragedy,
but these works were the productions of mature
masters, from whom things monumental and lasting
were expected as a matter of course; men like Wagner and Verdi. The generations had also seen the
coming of "Carmen" and gradually opened their
minds to an appreciation of its meaning and beauty,
while the youthful genius who had created it sank
almost unnoticed into his grave; but they had not
seen the advent of a work which almost in a day set
the world on fire and raised an unknown musician
from penury and obscurity to affluence and fame.
In the face of such an experience it was scarcely
to be wondered at that judgment was flung to the
winds and that the most volatile of musical nations
and the staidest alike hailed the young composer as
the successor of Verdi, the regenerator of operatic
Italy, and the pioneer of a new school which should
revitalize opera and make unnecessary the hopeless
task of trying to work along the lines laid down by
Wagner.

And this opera was the outcome of a competition
based on the frankest kind of commercialism — one
of those "occasionals" from which we have been
taught to believe we ought never to expect anything
of ideal and lasting merit. "Pagliacci" was, in a
way, a fruit of the same competition. Three years
before "Cavalleria rusticana" had started the
universal conflagration Ruggiero Leoncavallo, who

at sixteen years of age had won his diploma at the
Naples Conservatory and received the degree of
Doctor of Letters from the University of Bologna
at twenty, had read his dramatic poem "I Medici"
to the publisher Ricordi and been commissioned to
set it to music. For this work he was to receive
2400 francs. He completed the composition within
a year, but there was no contract that the opera
should be performed, and this hoped-for consumma-
tion did not follow. Then came Mascagni's triumph,
and Leoncavallo, who had been obliged meanwhile
to return to the routine work of an operatic *repétiteur*,
lost patience. Satisfied that Ricordi would never
do anything more for him, and become desperate,
he shut himself in his room to attempt "one more
work" — as he said in an autobiographical sketch
which appeared in "La Reforme," a journal published in Alexandria. In five months he had written
the book and music of "Pagliacci," which was
accepted for publication and production by Sonzogno,
Ricordi's business rival, after a single reading of
the poem. Maurel, whose friendship Leoncavallo
had made while coaching opera singers in Paris,
used his influence in favor of the opera, offered to
create the part of *Tonio*, and did so at the first performance of the opera at the Teatro dal Verme,
Milan, on May 17, 1892.

Leoncavallo's opera turns on a tragical ending to
a comedy which is incorporated in the play. The
comedy is a familiar one among the strolling players

who perform at village fairs in Italy, in which Colombina, Pagliaccio, and Arlecchino (respectively the Columbine, Clown, and Harlequin of our pantomime) take part. Pagliaccio is husband to Colombina and Arlecchino is her lover, who hoodwinks Pagliaccio. There is a fourth character, Taddeo, a servant, who makes foolish love to Columbina and, mingling imbecile stupidity with maliciousness, delights in the domestic discord which he helps to foment. The first act of the opera may be looked upon as an induction to the conventional comedy which comes to an unconventional and tragic end through the fact that the Clown (*Canio*) is in real life the husband of Columbine (*Nedda*) and is murderously jealous of her; wherefore, forgetting himself in a mad rage, he kills her and her lover in the midst of the mimic scene. The lover, however, is not the Harlequin of the comedy, but one of the spectators whom *Canio* had vainly sought to identify, but who is unconsciously betrayed by his mistress in her death agony. The Taddeo of the comedy is the clown of the company, who in real life entertains a passion for *Nedda*, which is repulsed, whereupon he also carries his part into actuality and betrays *Nedda's* secret to *Canio*. It is in the ingenious interweaving of these threads — the weft of reality with the warp of simulation — that the chief dramatic value of Leoncavallo's opera lies.

Actual murder by a man while apparently playing a part in a drama is older as a dramatic *motif* than

"Pagliacci," and Leoncavallo's employment of it
gave rise to an interesting controversy and a still more
interesting revelation in the early days of the opera.
Old theatre-goers in England and America remember
the device as it was employed in Dennery's "Pail-
laisse," known on the English stage as "Belphegor,
the Mountebank." In 1874 Paul Ferrier produced
a play entitled "Tabarin," in which Coquelin appeared at the Théâtre Français. Thirteen years
later Catulle Mendès brought out another play
called "La Femme de Tabarin," for which Chabrier
wrote the incidental music. The critics were prompt
in charging Mendès with having plagiarized Ferrier,
and the former defended himself on the ground that
the incident which he had employed, of actual
murder in a dramatic performance, was historical
and had often been used. This, however, did not
prevent him from bringing an accusation of theft
against Leoncavallo when "Pagliacci" was announced for production in French at Brussels and of
beginning legal proceedings against the composer
and his publisher on that score. The controversy
which followed showed very plainly that Mendès
did not have a leg to stand upon either in law or
equity, and he withdrew his suit and made a handsome *amende* in a letter to the editor of "Le Figaro."
Before this was done, however, Signor Leoncavallo
wrote a letter to his publisher, which not only established that the incident in question was based upon
fact but directed attention to a dramatic use of the

motif in a Spanish play written thirty-five years before the occurrence which was in the mind of Leoncavallo. The letter was as follows : —

Lugano, Sept. 3, 1894.

Dear Signor Sonzogno.

I have read Catulle Mendès's two letters. M. Mendès goes pretty far in declaring *a priori* that "Pagliacci" is an imitation of his "Femme de Tabarin." I had not known this book, and only know it now through the accounts given in the daily papers. You will remember that at the time of the first performance of "Pagliacci" at Milan in 1892 several critics accused me of having taken the subject of my opera from the "Drama Nuevo" of the well known Spanish writer, Estebanez. What would M. Mendès say if he were accused of having taken the plot of "La Femme de Tabarin" from the "Drama Nuevo," which dates back to 1830 or 1840? As a fact, a husband, a comedian, kills in the last scene the lover of his wife before her eyes while he only appears to play his part in the piece.

It is absolutely true that I knew at that time no more of the "Drama Nuevo" than I know now of "La Femme de Tabarin." I saw the first mentioned work in Rome represented by Novelli six months after "Pagliacci's" first production in Milan. In my childhood, while my father was judge at Montalto, in Calabria (the scene of the opera's plot), a jealous player killed his wife after the performance. This event made a deep and lasting impression on my childish mind, the more since my father was the judge at the criminal's trial ; and later, when I took up dramatic work, I used this episode for a drama. I left the frame of the piece as I saw it, and it can be seen now at the Festival of Madonna della Serra, at Montalto. The clowns arrive a week or ten days before the festival, which takes place on August 15, to put up their tents and booths in the open space which reaches from the church toward the fields. I have not even invented the coming of the peasants from Santo Benedetto, a neighboring village, during the chorale.

What I write now I have mentioned so often in Germany and other parts that several opera houses, notably that of Berlin, had printed on their bills "Scene of the true event." After all this, M. Mendès insisted on his claim, which means that he does not believe my words. Had I used M. Mendès's ideas I would not have hesitated to open correspondence with him before the first representation, as I have done now with a well known writer who has a subject that I wish to use for a future work. "Pagliacci" is my own, entirely my own. If in this opera, a scene reminds one of M. Mendès's book, it only proves that we both had the same idea which Estebanez had before us. On my honor and conscience I assure you that I have read but two of M. Mendès's books in my life — "Zo Hur" and "La Première Maîtresse." When I read at Marienbad a little while ago the newspaper notices on the production of "La Femme de Tabarin" I even wrote to you, dear Signor Sonzogno, thinking this was an imitation of "Pagliacci." This assertion will suffice, coming from an honorable man, to prove my loyalty. If not, then I will place my undoubted rights under the protection of the law, and furnish incontestable proof of what I have stated here.

I have the honor, etc., etc.

At various times and in various manners, by letters and in newspaper interviews, Leoncavallo reiterated the statement that the incident which he had witnessed as a boy in his father's courtroom had suggested his drama. The chief actor in the incident, he said, was still living. After conviction he was asked if he felt penitent. The rough voice which rang through the room years before still echoed in Leoncavallo's ears: "I repent me of nothing! On the contrary, if I had it to do over again I'd do it again!" (*Non mi pento del delitto! Tutt altro. Se dovessi ricominciare, ricomincerei!*) He was sentenced to imprisonment and after the expiration of his term took service in a little Calabrian town with Baroness Sproniere. If Mendès had prosecuted his action, "poor Alessandro" was ready to appear as a witness and tell the story which Leoncavallo had dramatized.

I have never seen "La Femme de Tabarin" and must rely on Mr. Philip Hale, fecund fountain of informal information, for an outline of the play which "Pagliacci" called back into public notice: Francisquine, the wife of Tabarin, irons her petticoats in the players' booth. A musketeer saunters along, stops and makes love to her. She listens greedily. Tabarin enters just after she has made an appointment with the man. Tabarin is drunk — drunker than usual. He adores his wife; he falls at her feet; he entreats her; he threatens her. Meanwhile the crowd gathers to see the "parade." Tabarin mounts the platform and tells openly of his jealousy. He calls his wife; she does not answer. He opens the curtain behind him; then he sees her in the arms of the musketeer. Tabarin snatches up a sword, stabs his wife in the breast and comes back to the stage with starting eyes and hoarse voice. The crowd marvels at the passion of his play. Francisquine, bloody, drags herself along the boards. She chokes; she cannot speak. Tabarin, mad with despair, gives her the sword, begs her to kill him. She seizes the sword, raises herself, hiccoughs, gasps out the word "Canaille," and dies before she can strike.

Paul Ferrier and Emanuel Pessard produced a grand opera in two acts entitled "Tabarin" in Paris in 1885; Alboiz and André a comic opera with the same title, music by Georges Bousquet, in 1852. Gilles and Furpilles brought out an operetta called "Tabarin Duelliste," with music by Léon Pillaut, in 1866. The works seem to have had only the name of the hero in common. Their stories bear no likeness to those of "La Femme de Tabarin" or "Pagliacci." The Spanish play, "Drama Nuevo," by Estebanez, was adapted for performance in English by Mr. W. D. Howells under the title "Yorick's Love." The translation was made for Mr. Lawrence Barrett and was never published in book form. If it had the dénouement suggested in Leoncavallo's letter to Sonzogno, the fact has escaped the memory of Mr. Howells, who, in answer to a letter of inquiry which I sent him, wrote: "So far as I can remember there was no likeness between 'Yorick's Love' and 'Pagliacci.' But when I made my version I had not seen or heard 'Pagliacci.'"

The title of Leoncavallo's opera is "Pagliacci," not "I Pagliacci" as it frequently appears in books

I

and newspapers.   When the opera was brought out
in the vernacular, Mr. Frederick E. Weatherly, who
made the English adaptation, called the play and
the character assumed by *Canio* in the comedy
"Punchinello."   This evoked an interesting comment from Mr. Hale: "'Pagliacci' is the plural
of Pagliaccio, which does not mean and never did
mean Punchinello.   What is a Pagliaccio?   A type
long known to the Italians, and familiar to the French
as Paillasse.   The Pagliaccio visited Paris first in
1570.   He was clothed in white and wore big buttons.
Later, he wore a suit of bedtick, with white and blue
checks, the coarse mattress cloth of the period.
Hence his name.   The word that meant straw was
afterward used for mattress which was stuffed with
straw and then for the buffoon, who wore the mattress
cloth suit.   In France the Paillasse, as I have said,
was the same as Pagliaccio.   Sometimes he wore a
red checked suit, but the genuine one was known by
the colors, white and blue.   He wore blue stockings,
short breeches puffing out *à la blouse*, a belted blouse
and a black, close-fitting cap.   This buffoon was seen
at shows of strolling mountebanks.   He stood outside the booth and by his jests and antics and grim-
aces strove to attract the attention of the people,
and he told them of the wonders performed by
acrobats within, of the freaks exhibited.   Many of
his jests are preserved.   They are often in dialogue
with the proprietor and are generally of vile in-
decency.   The lowest of the strollers, he was abused

by them. The Italian Pagliaccio is a species of
clown, and Punchinello was never a mere buffoon.
The Punch of the puppet-show is a bastard descen-
dant of the latter, but the original type is still seen
in Naples, where he wears a white costume and a
black mask. The original type was not necessarily
humpbacked. Punchinello is a shrewd fellow, intellectual, yet in touch with the people, cynical; not
hesitating at murder if he can make by it; at the
same time a local satirist, a dealer in gags and quips.
Pagliacci is perhaps best translated by 'clowns';
but the latter word must not be taken in its restricted circus sense. These strolling clowns are
pantomimists, singers, comedians."

At the first performance of "Pagliacci" in Milan
the cast was as follows: *Canio*, Geraud; *Tonio*,
Maurel; *Silvio*, Ancona; *Peppe*, Daddi; *Nedda*,
Mme. Stehle. The first performance in America was
by the Hinrichs Grand Opera Company, at the Grand
Opera House, New York, on June 15, 1893; Selma
Kronold was the *Nedda*, Montegriffo the *Canio*, and
Campanari the *Tonio*. The opera was incorporated
in the Metropolitan repertory in the season of 1893–
1894.

*

* *

Rinuccini's "Dafne," which was written 300
years ago and more, begins with a prologue which
was spoken in the character of the poet Ovid. Leoncavallo's "Pagliacci" also begins with a prologue,

but it is spoken by one of the people of the play; whether in his character as *Tonio* of the tragedy or *Pagliaccio* of the comedy there is no telling. He speaks the sentiments of the one and wears the motley of the other. Text and music, however, are ingeniously contrived to serve as an index to the purposes of the poet and the method and material of the composer. In his speech the prologue tells us that the author of the play is fond of the ancient custom of such an introduction, but not of the old purpose. He does not employ it for the purpose of proclaiming that the tears and passions of the actors are but simulated and false. No! He wishes to let us know that his play is drawn from life as it is — that it is true. It welled up within him when memories of the past sang in his heart and was written down to show us that actors are human beings like unto ourselves.

An unnecessary preachment, and if listened to with a critical disposition rather an impertinence, as calculated to rob us of the pleasure of illusion which it is the province of the drama to give. Closely analyzed, *Tonio's* speech is very much of a piece with the prologue which *Bully Bottom* wanted for the play of "Pyramus" in Shakespeare's comedy. We are asked to see a play. In this play there is another play. In this other play one of the actors plays at cross-purposes with the author — forgets his lines and himself altogether and becomes in reality the man that he seems to be in the first play.

The prologue deliberately aims to deprive us of the thrill of surprise at the unexpected dénouement, simply that he may tell us what we already know as well as he, that an actor is a human being.

Plainly then, from a didactic point of view, this prologue is a gratuitous impertinence. Not so its music. Structurally, it is little more than a loose-jointed pot-pourri; but it serves the purpose of a thematic catalogue to the chief melodic incidents of the play which is to follow. In this it bears a faint resemblance to the introduction to Berlioz's "Romeo and Juliet" symphony. It begins with an energetic figure,

which is immediately followed by an upward scale-passage with a saucy flourish at the end — not unlike the crack of a whiplash: —

It helps admirably to picture the bustling activity of the *festa* into which we are soon to be precipitated.

The bits of melody which are now introduced might all be labelled in the Wolzogen-Wagner manner with reference to the play's peoples and their passions if it were worth while to do so, or if their beauty and eloquence were not sufficient unto themselves. First we have the phrase in which *Canio* will tell us how a clown's heart must seem merry and make laughter though it be breaking : —

Next the phrase from the love music of *Nedda* and *Silvio* : —

The bustling music returns, develops great energy, then pauses, hesitates, and makes way for *Tonio*, who, putting his head through the curtain, politely asks permission of the audience, steps forward and delivers his homily, which is alternately declamatory and broadly melodious. One of his melodies later becomes the theme of the between-acts music, which separates the supposedly real life of the strolling players from the comedy which they present to the mimic audience : —

Ah think then, sweet peo - ple, when ye
E - vo *piut - to - sto* *che* *le*

look on us clad in our mot - ley
no - stre po *ve - re gab - ba* *ne*

At last *Tonio* calls upon his fellow mountebanks to begin their play. The curtain rises. We are in the midst of a rural celebration of the Feast of the Assumption on the outskirts of a village in Calabria. A perambulant theatre has been set up among the trees and the strolling actors are arriving, accompanied by a crowd of villagers, who shout greetings to Clown, Columbine, and Harlequin. *Nedda* arrives in a cart drawn by a donkey led by *Beppe*. *Canio* in character invites the crowd to come to the show at 7 o'clock (*ventitre ore*). There they shall be regaled with a sight of the domestic troubles of Pagliaccio and see the fat mischief-maker tremble. *Tonio* wants to help *Nedda* out of the cart, but *Canio* interferes and lifts her down himself ; whereupon the women and boys twit *Tonio*. *Canio* and *Beppe*

wet their whistles at the tavern, but *Tonio* remains
behind on the plea that he must curry the donkey.
The hospitable villager playfully suggests that it is
Tonio's purpose to make love to *Nedda*. *Canio*,
half in earnest, half in jest, points out the difference
between real life and the stage.   In the play, if he
catches a lover with his wife, he flies into a mock
passion, preaches a sermon, and takes a drubbing
from the swain to the amusement of the audience.
But there would be a different ending to the story
were *Nedda* actually to deceive him.   Let *Tonio*
beware!   Does he doubt *Nedda's* fidelity?   Not at
all.   He loves her and seals his assurance with a
kiss.   Then off to the tavern.

Hark to the bagpipes!   Huzza, here come the
zampognari!   Drone pipes droning and chaunters
skirling — as well as they can skirl in Italian!

Now we have people and pipers on the stage and
there's a bell in the steeple ringing for vespers.
Therefore a chorus.   Not that we have anything to
say that concerns the story in any way.   "Din,
don!"   That would suffice, but if you must have
more: "Let's to church.   Din, don.   All's right
with love and the sunset.   Din, don!   But mamma
has her eye on the young folk and their inclination

for kissing. Din, don!'" Bells and pipes are echoed by the singers.

Her husband is gone to the tavern for refreshment and *Nedda* is left alone. There is a little trouble in her mind caused by the fierceness of *Canio's* voice and looks. Does he suspect? But why yield to such fancies and fears? How beautiful the mid-August sun is! Her hopes and longings find expression in the Ballatella — a waltz tune with twitter of birds and rustle of leaves for accompaniment. Pretty birds, where are you going? What is it you say? Mother knew your song and used once to tell it to her babe. How your wings flash through the ether! Heedless of cloud and tempest, on, on, past the stars, and still on! Her wishes take flight with the feathered songsters, but *Tonio* brings her rudely to earth. He pleads for a return of the love which he says he bears her, but she bids him postpone his protestations till he can make them in the play. He grows desperately urgent and attempts to rape a kiss. She cuts him across the face with a donkey whip, and he goes away blaspheming and swearing vengeance.

Then *Silvio* comes — *Silvio*, the villager, who loves her and who has her heart. She fears he will be discovered, but he bids her be at peace; he had left *Canio* drinking at the tavern. She tells him of the scene with *Tonio* and warns him, but he laughs at her fears. Then he pleads with her. She does not love her husband; she is weary of the wandering

life which she is forced to lead; if her love is true
let her fly with him to happiness. No. 'Tis folly,
madness; her heart is his, but he must not tempt
her to its destruction. *Tonio* slinks in and plays
eavesdropper. He hears the mutual protestations
of the lovers, hears *Nedda* yield to *Silvio's* wild pleadings, sees them locked in each other's arms, and hurries off to fetch *Canio*. *Canio* comes, but not in time
to see the man who had climbed over the wall, yet
in time to hear *Nedda's* word of parting: *A stanotte*
— *e per sempre tua saro* — "To-night, and forever,
I am yours!" He throws *Nedda* aside and gives
chase after the fugitive, but is baffled. He demands
to be told the name of her lover. *Nedda* refuses to
answer. He rushes upon her with dagger drawn,
but *Beppe* intercepts and disarms him. There is
haste now; the villagers are already gathering for
the play. *Tonio* insinuates his wicked advice: Let
us dissemble; the gallant may be caught at the play.
The others go out to prepare for their labors. *Canio*
staggers toward the theatre. He must act the merry
fool, though his heart be torn! Why not? What
is he? A man? No; a clown! On with the
motley! The public must be amused. What
though Harlequin steals his Columbine? Laugh,
Pagliaccio, though thy heart break!

The between-acts music is retrospective; it comments on the tragic emotions, the pathos foretold
in the prologue. Act II brings the comedy which is
to have a realistic and bloody ending. The villagers

gather and struggle for places in front of the booth.
Among them is *Silvio,* to whom *Nedda* speaks a word
of warning as she passes him while collecting the
admission fees.   He reminds her of the assignation ;
she will be there.   The comedy begins to the music
of a graceful minuet : —

Columbine is waiting for Harlequin.   Taddeo is
at the market buying the supper for the mimic lovers.
Harlequin sings his serenade under the window:
"O, Colombina, il tenero fido Arlecchin" — a pretty
measure !   Taddeo enters and pours out his admiration for Colombina in an exaggerated cadenza as
he offers her his basket of purchases.   The audience
shows enjoyment of the sport.   Taddeo makes love
to Colombina and Harlequin, entering by the window, lifts him up by the ears from the floor where he
is kneeling and kicks him out of the room.   What
fun !   The mimic lovers sit at table and discuss the
supper and their love.   Taddeo enters in mock alarm
to tell of the coming of Pagliaccio.   Harlequin

decamps, but leaves a philtre in the hands of Columbine to be poured into her husband's wine.   At the
window Columbine calls after him : *A stanotte —
e per sempre io saro tua!*   At this moment *Canio*
enters in the character of Pagliaccio.   He hears
again the words which *Nedda* had called after the
fleeing *Silvio*, and for a moment is startled out of his
character.   But he collects himself and begins to
play his part.   "A man has been here !"   "You've
been drinking !"   The dialogue of the comedy continues, but ever and anon with difficulty on the part
of Pagliaccio, who begins to put a sinister inflection
into his words.   Taddeo is dragged from the cup-
board in which he had taken hiding.   He, too, puts
color of verity into his lines, especially when he prates
about the purity of Columbine.   *Canio* loses control
of himself more and more.   "Pagliaccio no more,
but a man — a man seeking vengeance.   The name
of your lover !"   The audience is moved by his
intensity.   *Silvio* betrays anxiety.   *Canio* rages on.
"The name, the name !"   The mimic audience
shouts, "Bravo !"   *Nedda :* if he doubts her she will
go.   "No, by God !   You'll remain and tell me the
name of your lover !"   With a great effort *Nedda*
forces herself to remain in character.   The music,
whose tripping dance measures have given way to
sinister mutterings in keeping with *Canio's* mad out-
bursts, as the mimic play ever and anon threatens
to leave its grooves and plunge into the tragic vortex
of reality, changes to a gavotte : —

Columbine explains: she had no idea her husband could put on so tragical a mask. It is only harmless Harlequin who has been her companion. "The name! *The name!!* THE NAME!!!" *Nedda* sees catastrophe approaching and throws her character to the winds. She shrieks out a defiant "No!" and attempts to escape from the mimic stage. *Silvio* starts up with dagger drawn. The spectators rise in confusion and cry "Stop him!" *Canio* seizes *Nedda* and plunges his knife into her: "Take that! And that! With thy dying gasps thou'lt tell me!" Woful intuition! Dying, *Nedda* calls: "Help, Silvio!" *Silvio* rushes forward and receives *Canio's* knife in his heart. "Gesumaria!" shriek the women. Men throw themselves upon *Canio.* He stands for a moment in a stupor, drops his knife and speaks the words: "The comedy is ended." "Ridi Pagliaccio!" shrieks the orchestra as the curtain falls.

"Plaudite, amici," said Beethoven on his death bed, "la commedia finita est!" And there is a tradition that these, too, were the last words of the

arch-jester Rabelais. "When 'Pagliacci' was first
sung here (in Boston), by the Tavary company,"
says Mr. Philip Hale, "*Tonio* pointed to the dead
bodies and uttered the sentence in a mocking way.
And there is a report that such was Leoncavallo's
original intention. As the *Tonio* began the piece in
explanation so he should end it. But the tenor
(de Lucia) insisted that he should speak the line.
I do not believe the story. (1) As Maurel was the
original *Tonio* and the tenor was comparatively
unknown, it is doubtful whether Maurel, of all men,
would have allowed of the loss of a fat line. (2) As
Canio is chief of the company it is eminently proper
that he should make the announcement to the crowd.
(3) The ghastly irony is accentuated by the speech
when it comes from *Canio's* mouth."

CHAPTER IX

"CAVALLERIA RUSTICANA"

HAVING neither the patience nor the inclination to paraphrase a comment on Mascagni's "Cavalleria rusticana" which I wrote years ago when the opera was comparatively new, and as it appears to me to contain a just estimate and criticism of the work and the school of which it and "Pagliacci" remain the foremost exemplars, I quote from my book, "Chapters of Opera"[1]: "Seventeen years ago 'Cavalleria rusticana' had no perspective. Now, though but a small portion of its progeny has been brought to our notice, we nevertheless look at it through a vista which looks like a valley of moral and physical death through which there flows a sluggish stream thick with filth and red with blood. Strangely enough, in spite of the consequences which have followed it, the fierce little drama retains its old potency. It still speaks with a voice which sounds like the voice of truth. Its music still makes the nerves tingle, and carries our feelings unresistingly on its turbulent current. But the stage-picture is less sanguinary than it looked in the beginning. It

---

[1] "Chapters of Opera," by H. E. Krehbiel, p. 223.

127

seems to have receded a millennium in time. It
has the terrible fierceness of an Attic tragedy, but
it also has the decorum which the Attic tragedy
never violated.   There is no slaughter in the presence
of the audience, despite the humbleness of its personages.   It does not keep us perpetually in sight of the
shambles.   It is, indeed, an exposition of chivalry;
rustic, but chivalry nevertheless.   It was thus Clytemnestra slew her husband, and Orestes his mother.
Note the contrast which the duel between *Alfio* and
Turiddu presents with the double murder to the
piquant accompaniment of comedy in 'Pagliacci,'
the opera which followed so hard upon its heels.
Since then piquancy has been the cry; the piquant
contemplation of adultery, seduction, and murder
amid the reek and stench of the Italian barnyard.
Think of Cilèa's 'Tilda,' Giordano's 'Mala Vita,'
Spinelli's 'A Basso Porto,' and Tasca's 'A Santa
Lucia'!

"The stories chosen for operatic treatment by the
champions of *verismo* are all alike.   It is their filth
and blood which fructifies the music, which rasps
the nerves even as the plays revolt the moral stomach.
I repeat: Looking back over the time during which
this so-called veritism has held its orgies, 'Cavalleria
rusticana' seems almost classic.   Its music is highly
spiced and tastes 'hot i' th' mouth,' but its eloquence
is, after all, in its eager, pulsating, passionate melody
— like the music which Verdi wrote more than half
a century ago for the last act of 'Il Trovatore.'   If

neither Mascagni himself nor his imitators have succeeded in equalling it since, it is because they have thought too much of the external devices of abrupt and uncouth change of modes and tonalities, of exotic scales and garish orchestration, and too little of the fundamental element of melody which once was the be-all and end-all of Italian music. Another fountain of gushing melody must be opened before 'Cavalleria rusticana' finds a successor in all things worthy of the succession. Ingenious artifice, reflection, and technical cleverness will not suffice even with the blood and mud of the slums as a fertilizer."

How Mascagni came to write his opera he has himself told us in a bright sketch of the early part of his life-history which was printed in the "Fanfulla della Domenica" of Rome shortly after he became famous. Recounting the story of his struggle for existence after entering upon his career, he wrote : —

In 1888 only a few scenes (of "Ratcliff") remained to be composed; but I let them lie and have not touched them since. The thought of "Cavalleria rusticana" had been in my head for several years. I wanted to introduce myself with a work of small dimensions. I appealed to several librettists, but none was willing to undertake the work without a guarantee of recompense. Then came notice of the Sonzogno competition and I eagerly seized the opportunity to better my condition. But my salary of 100 lire, to which nothing was added, except the fees from a few pianoforte lessons in Cerignola and two lessons in the Philharmonic Society of Canosa (a little town a

K

few miles from Cerignola), did not permit the luxury of a libretto. At the solicitation of some friends Targioni, in Leghorn, decided to write a "Cavalleria rusticana" for me. My mind was long occupied with the finale. The words: *Hanno ammazzato compare Turiddu!* (They have killed Neighbor Turiddu!) were forever ringing in my ears. I needed a few mighty orchestral chords to give characteristic form to the musical phrase and achieve an impressive close. How it happened I don't know, but one morning, as I was trudging along the road to give my lessons at Canosa, the idea came to me like a stroke of lightning, and I had found my chords. They were those seventh chords, which I conscientiously set down in my manuscript.

Thus I began my opera at the end. When I received the first chorus of my libretto by post (I composed the Siciliano in the prelude later) I said in great good humor to my wife:

"To-day we must make a large expenditure."

"What for?"

"An alarm clock."

"Why?"

"To wake me up before dawn so that I may begin to write on 'Cavalleria rusticana.'"

The expenditure caused a dubious change in the monthly budget, but it was willingly allowed. We went out together, and after a good deal of bargaining spent nine lire. I am sure that I can find the clock, all safe and sound, in Cerignola. I wound it up the evening we bought it, but it was destined to be of no service to me, for in that night a son, the first of a row of them, was born to me. In spite of this I carried out my determination, and in the morning began to write the first chorus of "Cavalleria." I came to Rome in February, 1890, in order to permit the jury to hear my opera; they decided that it was worthy of performance. Returning to Cerignola in a state of the greatest excitement, I noticed that I did not have a penny in my pocket for the return trip to Rome when my opera was to be rehearsed. Signor Sonzogno helped me out of my embarrassment with a few hundred francs.

Those beautiful days of fear and hope, of discouragement and confidence, are as vividly before my eyes as if they were now. I see again the Constanzi Theatre, half filled; I see how, after the last excited measures of the orchestra, they all raise their arms and gesticulate, as if they were threatening me; and in my soul there awakens an echo of that cry of approval which almost prostrated me. The effect made upon me was so powerful that at the second representation I had to request them to turn down the footlights in case I should be called out; for the blinding light seemed a hell to me, like a fiery abyss that threatened to engulf me.

It is a rude little tale which Giovanni Verga wrote and which supplied the librettists, G. Targioni-Tozzetti and G. Menasci, with the plot of Mascagni's opera. Sententious as the opera seems, it is yet puffed out, padded, and bedizened with unessential ornament compared with the story. This has the simplicity and directness of a folk-tale or folk-song, and much of its characteristic color and strength were lost in fitting it out for music. The play, which Signora Duse presented to us with a power which no operatic singer can ever hope to match, was more to the purpose, quicker and stronger in movement, fiercer in its onrush of passion, and more pathetic in its silences than the opera with its music, though the note of pathos sounded by Signor Mascagni is the most admirable element of the score. With half a dozen homely touches Verga conjures up the life of a Sicilian village and strikes out his characters in bold outline. Turiddu Macca, son of Nunzia, is a *bersagliere* returned from service. He struts about the village streets in his uniform, smoking a pipe carved with an image of the king on horseback, which he lights with a match fired by a scratch on the seat of his trousers, "lifting his leg as if for a kick." Lola, daughter of Massaro Angelo, was his sweetheart when he was conscripted, but meanwhile she has promised to marry Alfio, a teamster from Licodia, who has four Sortino mules in his stable. Now Turiddu could do nothing better than sing spiteful songs under her window.

Lola married the teamster, and on Sundays she would sit in the yard with her hands posed on her hips to show off the thick gold rings which her husband had given her. Opposite Alfio's house lived Massaro Cola, who was as rich as a hog, as they said, and who had an only daughter named Santa. Turiddu, to spite Lola, paid his addresses to Santa and whispered sweet words into her ear.

"Why don't you go and say these nice things to Lola?" asked Santa one day.

"Lola is a fine lady now; she has married a crown prince. But you are worth a thousand Lolas; she isn't worthy of wearing your old shoes. I could just eat you up with my eyes, Santa"—thus Turiddu.

"You may eat me with your eyes and welcome, for then there will be no leaving of crumbs."

"If I were rich I would like to have a wife just like you."

"I shall never marry a crown prince, but I shall have a dowry as well as Lola when the good Lord sends me a lover."

The tassel on his cap had tickled the girl's fancy. Her father disapproved of the young soldier, and turned him from his door; but Santa opened her window to him until the village gossips got busy with her name and his. Lola listened to the talk of the lovers from behind a vase of flowers. One day she called after Turiddu: "Ah, Turiddu! Old friends are no longer noticed, eh?"

"He is a happy man who has the chance of seeing you, Lola."

"You know where I live," answered Lola. And now Turiddu visited Lola so often that Santa shut her window in his face and the villagers began to smile knowingly when he passed by. Alfio was making a round of the fairs with his mules. "Next Sunday I must go to confession," said Lola one day, "for last night I dreamt that I saw black grapes."

"Never mind the dream," pleaded Turiddu.

"But Easter is coming, and my husband will want to know why I have not confessed."

Santa was before the confessional waiting her turn when Lola was receiving absolution. "I wouldn't send you to Rome for absolution," she said. Alfio came home with his mules, and money and a rich holiday dress for his wife.

"You do well to bring presents to her," said Santa to him, "for when you are away your wife adorns your head for you."

"Holy Devil!" screamed Alfio. "Be sure of what you are saying, or I'll not leave you an eye to cry with!"

"I am not in the habit of crying. I haven't wept even when I have seen Turiddu going into your wife's house at night."

"Enough!" said Alfio. "I thank you very much."

The cat having come back home, Turiddu kept off the streets by day, but in the evenings consoled himself with his friends at the tavern. They were enjoying a dish of sausages there on Easter eve. When Alfio came in Turiddu understood what he wanted by the way he fixed his eyes on him. "You know what I want to speak to you about," said Alfio when Turiddu asked him if he had any commands to give him. He offered Alfio a glass of wine, but it was refused with a wave of the hand.

"Here I am," said Turiddu. Alfio put his arms around his neck. "We'll talk this thing over if you will meet me to-morrow morning."

"You may look for me on the highway at sunrise, and we will go on together."

They exchanged the kiss of challenge, and Turiddu, as an earnest that he would be on hand, bit Alfio's ear. His companions left their sausages uneaten and went home with Turiddu. There his mother was sitting up for him.

, "Mamma," Turridu said to her, "do you remember that when I went away to be a soldier you thought I would never come back? Kiss me as you did then, mamma, for to-morrow I am going away again."

Before daybreak he took his knife from the place in the haymow where he had hidden it when he went soldiering, and went out to meet Alfio.

"Holy Mother of Jesus!" grumbled Lola when her husband prepared to go out; "where are you going in such a hurry?"

"I am going far away," answered Alfio, "and it will be better for you if I never come back!"

The two men met on the highway and for a while walked on in silence. Turiddu kept his cap pulled down over his face. "Neighbor Alfio," he said after a space, "as true as I live I know that I have wronged you, and I would let myself be killed if I had not seen my old mother when she got up on the pretext of looking after the hens. And now, as true as I live, I will kill you like a dog so that my dear old mother may not have cause to weep."

"Good!" answered Alfio; "we will both strike hard!" And he took off his coat.

Both were good with the knife. Turiddu received the first blow in his arm, and when he returned it struck for Alfio's heart.

"Ah, Turiddu! You really do intend to kill me?"

"Yes, I told you so. Since I saw her in the hen-yard I have my old mother always in my eyes."

"Keep those eyes wide open," shouted Alfio, "for I am going to return you good measure!"

Alfio crouched almost to the ground, keeping his left hand on the wound, which pained him. Suddenly he seized a handful of dust and threw it into Turiddu's eyes.

"Ah!" howled Turiddu, blinded by the dust, "I'm a dead man!" He attempted to save himself by leaping backward, but Alfio struck him a second blow, this time in the belly, and a third in the throat.

"That makes three — the last for the head you have adorned for me!"

Turiddu staggered back into the bushes and fell. He tried to say, "Ah, my dear mother!" but the blood gurgled up in his throat and he could not.

Music lends itself incalculably better to the celebration of a mood accomplished or achieved by action, physical or psychological, than to an expression of the action itself. It is in the nature of the lyric drama that this should be so, and there need be no wonder that wherever Verga offered an opportunity for set lyricism it was embraced by Mascagni and his librettists. Verga tells us that Turiddu, having lost Lola, comforted himself by singing spiteful songs under her window. This suggested the Siciliano, which, an afterthought, Mascagni put into his prelude as a serenade, not in disparagement, but in praise of Lola. It was at Easter that Alfio returned to discover the infidelity of his wife, and hence we have an Easter hymn, one of the musical high lights of the work, though of no dramatic value. Verga aims to awaken at least a tittle of extenuation and a spark of sympathy for Turiddu by showing us his filial love in conflict with his willingness to make reparation to Alfio; Mascagni and his librettists do more by showing us the figure of the young soldier blending a request for a farewell kiss from his mother with a prayer for protection for the woman he has wronged. In its delineation of the tender emotions, indeed, the opera is more generous and kindly than the story. *Santuzza* does not betray her lover in cold blood as does Santa, but in the depth of her humiliation and at the climax of her jealous fury created by *Turiddu's* rejection of her when he follows *Lola* into church. Moreover, her love opens the gates to remorse the moment she realizes what the consequence of her act is to be. The opera sacrifices some of the virility of Turiddu's character as sketched by Verga, but by its classic treatment of the scene of the killing it saves us from the contemplation of Alfio's dastardly trick which turns a duel into a cowardly assassination.

The prelude to the opera set the form which Leoncavallo followed, slavishly followed, in "Pagliacci."

The orchestral proclamation of the moving passions
of the play is made by the use of fragments of melody
which in the vocal score mark climaxes in the dialogue.   The first high point in the prelude is reached
in the strain to which *Santuzza* begs for the love of
Turiddu, even after she has disclosed to him her
knowledge of his infidelity : —

the second is the broad melody in which she pleads with him to return to her arms:—

Between these expositions falls the Siciliano, which interrupts the instrumental flood just as *Lola's* careless song, the Stornello, interrupts the passionate rush of *Santuzza's* protestations, prayers, and lamentations in the scene between her and her faithless lover : —

O   Lo - la, bian-ca   co - me flor di spi - no . .
quan-do t'af - fac - ci   te   s'affaccio il   so - le,

These sharp contrasts, heightened by the device of surprise, form one of the marked characteristics of Mascagni's score and one of the most effective. We meet it also in the instrumentation — the harp accompaniment to the serenade, the pauses which give piquancy to *Lola's* ditty, the unison violins, harp arpeggios, and sustained organ chords of the intermezzo.

When the curtain rises it discloses the open square of a Sicilian village, flanked by a church and the inn of *Lucia, Turiddu's* mother. It is Easter morning and villagers and peasants are gathering for the Paschal mass. Church bells ring and the orchestra breaks into the eager melody which a little later we hear combined with the voices which are hymning the pleasant sights and sounds of nature :—

A charming conception is the regular beat and flux and reflux of the women's voices as they sing

Delightful and refreshing is the bustling strain of the men. The singers depart with soft exclamations of rapture called out by the contemplation of nature and thoughts of the Virgin Mother and Child in their hearts. Comes *Santuzza*, sore distressed, to *Mamma Lucia*, to inquire as to the whereabouts of her son *Turiddu*. *Lucia* thinks him at Francofonte; but *Santuzza* knows that he spent the night in the village.

In pity for the maiden's distress, *Lucia* asks her to enter her home, but *Santuzza* may not — she is excommunicate. *Alfio* enters with boisterous jollity, singing of his jovial carefree life as a teamster and his love of home and a faithful wife. It is a paltry measure, endurable only for its offering of contrast, and we will not tarry with it, though the villagers echo it merrily. *Alfio*, too, has seen *Turiddu*, and *Lucia* is about to express her surprise when *Santuzza* checks her. The hour of devotion is come, and the choir in the church intones the "Regina cœli," while the people without fall on their knees and sing the Resurrection Hymn. After the first outburst, to which the organ appends a brief postlude, *Santuzza* leads in the canticle, "Innegiamo il Signor non è morte":

Let us sing of our Lord ris'n victorious !
Let us sing of our Lord ever glorious : —

mor - to,   in - neg - gia . . . . . mo al Si -

gno - re   ri - sor - - to,

The instrumental basses supply a foundation of Bachian granite, the chorus within the church inter- polates shouts of "Alleluia!" and the song swells until the gates of sound fly wide open and we forget the theatre in a fervor of religious devotion. Only the critic in his study ought here to think of the parallel scene which Leoncavallo sought to create in his opera.

Thus far the little dramatic matter that has been

introduced is wholly expository; yet we are already
near the middle of the score. All the stage folk
enter the church save *Santuzza* and *Lucia,* and to
the mother of her betrayer the maiden tells the
story of her wrongs. The romance which she sings
is marked by the copious use of one of the distinguishing devices of the veritist composers — the
melodic triplet, an efficient help for the pushing,
pulsating declamation with which the dramatic
dialogue of Mascagni, Leoncavallo, and their fellows
is carried on. *Lucia* can do no more for the unfortunate than commend her to the care of the Virgin.
She enters the church and *Turiddu* comes. He lies
as to where he has been. *Santuzza* is quick with
accusation and reproach, but at the first sign of his
anger and a hint of the vengeance which *Alfio* will
take she abases herself. Let him beat and insult
her, she will love and pardon though her heart break.
She is in the extremity of agony and anguish when
Lola is heard trolling a careless song: —

Fior di giag - gio - lo. . . gli an-ge - li bel - li

stan - no a mil - le in cie - lo. . .

She is about to begin a second stanza when she
enters and sees the pair. She stops with an excla-

mation. She says she is seeking *Alfio*. Is *Turiddu* not going to mass? *Santuzza*, significantly: "It is Easter and the Lord sees all things! None but the blameless should go to mass." But *Lola* will go, and so will *Turiddu*. Scorning *Santuzza's* pleadings and at last hurling her to the ground, he rushes into the church. She shouts after him a threat of Easter vengeance and fate sends the agent to her in the very moment. *Alfio* comes and *Santuzza* tells him that *Turiddu* has cuckolded him and *Lola* has robbed her of her lover : —

> Turiddu mi tolse, mi tolse l'onore,
> E vostra moglie lui rapiva a me !

The oncoming waves of the drama's pathos have risen to a supreme height, their crests have broken, and the wind-blown spume drenches the soul of the listeners; but the composer has not departed from the first principle of the master of whom, for a time, it was hoped he might be the legitimate successor. Melody remains the life-blood of his music as it is that of Verdi's from his first work to his last; — as it will be so long as music endures.

Terrible is the outbreak of Alfio's rage : —

> Infami lero, ad esse non perdono,
> Vendetta avro pria che tra monti il di.

L

ad   és - - - - si   non per -

do - - no,   ven-det - ta   avró,

etc.

Upon this storm succeeds the calm of the intermezzo — in its day the best abused and most hack-
neyed piece of music that the world knew; yet a
triumph of simple, straightforward tune. It echoes
the Easter hymn, and in the midst of the tumult of
earthly passion proclaims celestial peace. Its instrumentation was doubtless borrowed from Hell-

mesberger's arrangement of the air "Ombra mai
fù" from "Serse," known the world over as Handel's
"Largo" — violins in unison, harp arpeggios, and
organ harmonies. In nothing artistically distin-
guished it makes an unexampled appeal to the multitude. Some years ago a burlesque on "Cavalleria
rusticana" was staged at a theatre in Vienna. It

was part of the witty conceit of the author to have
the intermezzo played on a handorgan. Up to this
point the audience had been hilarious in its enjoyment of the burlesque, but with the first wheezy
tones from the grinder the people settled down to
silent attention ; and when the end came applause for
the music rolled out wave after wave. A burlesque
performance could not rob that music of its charm.

Ite missa est. Mass is over. The merry music of
the first chorus returns. The worshippers are about
to start homeward with pious reflections, when
Turiddu detains *Lola* and invites his neighbors to a
glass of *Mamma Lucia's* wine. We could spare the
drinking song as easily as *Alfio*, entering, turns aside
the cup which *Turiddu* proffers him. *Turiddu*
understands. "I await your pleasure." Some of
the women apprehend mischief and lead *Lola* away.
The challenge is given and accepted, Sicilian fashion.
Turiddu confesses his wrong-doing to *Alfio*, but, instead of proclaiming his purpose to kill his enemy,
he asks protection for *Santuzza* in case of his death.
Then, while the violins tremble and throb, he calls
for his mother like an errant child: —

He has been too free with the winecup, he says, and
must leave her. But first her blessing, as when he
went away to be a soldier. Should he not return,
Santa must be her care: "Voi dovrete fare; da

madre a Santa !" It is the cry of a child. "A kiss !
Another kiss, mamma ! Farewell !" *Lucia* calls after
him. He is gone, *Santuzza* comes in with her phrase
of music descriptive of her unhappy love. It grows
to a thunderous crash. Then a hush ! A fateful
chord ! A whispered roll of the drums ! A woman
is heard to shriek: "They have killed Neighbor
Turiddu !" A crowd of women rush in excitedly;
Santuzza and *Lucia* fall in a swoon. "Hanno ammazzato compare Turiddu !" The tragedy is ended.

CHAPTER X

IT would be foolish to question or attempt to deny the merits of the type of Italian opera established by Mascagni's lucky inspiration. The brevity of the realistic little tragedy, the swiftness of its movement, its adherence to the Italian ideal of melody first, its ingenious combination of song with an illuminative orchestral part—these elements in union created a style which the composers of Italy, France, and Germany were quick to adopt. "Pagliacci" was the first fruit of the movement and has been the most enduring; indeed, so far as America and England are concerned, "Cavalleria rusticana" and "Pagliacci" are the only products of the school which have obtained a lasting footing. They were followed by a flood of Italian, French, and German works in which low life was realistically portrayed, but, though the manner of composition was as easily copied as the subjects were found in the slums, none of the imitators of Mascagni and Leoncavallo achieved even a tithe of their success. The men themselves were too shrewd and wise to attempt to repeat the experiment which had once been triumphant.

150

In one respect the influence of the twin operas was deplorable. I have attempted to characterize that influence in general terms, but in order that the lesson may be more plainly presented it seems to me best to present a few examples in detail. The eagerness with which writers sought success in moral muck, regardless of all artistic elements, is strikingly illustrated in an attempt by a German writer, Edmund von Freihold,[1] to provide "Cavalleria rusticana" with a sequel. Von Freihold wrote the libretto for a "music drama" which he called "Santuzza," the story of which begins long enough after the close of Verga's story for both the women concerned in "Cavalleria rusticana" to have grown children. *Santuzza* has given birth to a son named *Massimo*, and *Lola* to a daughter, *Anita*. The youthful pair grow up side by side in the Sicilian village and fall in love with one another. They might have married and in a way expiated the sins of their parents had not *Alfio* overheard his wife, *Lola*, confess that *Turiddu*, not her husband, is the father of *Anita*. The lovers are thus discovered to be half brother and sister. This reminder of his betrayal by *Lola* infuriates *Alfio* anew. He rushes upon his wife to kill her, but *Santuzza*, who hates him as the slayer of her lover, throws herself between and plunges her dagger in *Alfio's* heart. Having thus taken revenge for *Turiddu's* death, *Santuzza* dies out of hand, *Lola*, as an inferior character, falls

[1] I owe this illustration to Ferdinand Pfohl's book "Die Moderne Oper."

in a faint, and *Massimo* makes an end of the delectable
story by going away from there to parts unknown.

In Cilèa's "Tilda" a street singer seeks to avenge
her wrongs upon a faithless lover. She bribes a
jailor to connive at the escape of a robber whom he
is leading to capital punishment. This robber she
elects to be the instrument of her vengeance. Right
merrily she lives with him and his companions in
the greenwood until the band captures the renegade
lover on his wedding journey. *Tilda* rushes upon
the bride with drawn dagger, but melts with com-
passion when she sees her victim in the attitude of
prayer. She sinks to her knees beside her, only to
receive the death-blow from her seducer. There
are piquant contrasts in this picture and Ave
Marias and tarantellas in the music.

Take the story of Giordano's "Mala Vita."
Here the hero is a young dyer whose dissolute
habits have brought on tuberculosis of the lungs.
The principal object of his amours is the wife of a
friend. A violent hemorrhage warns him of approaching death. Stricken with fear he rushes to
the nearest statue of the Madonna and registers a
vow ; he will marry a wanton, effect her redemption,
thereby hoping to save his own miserable life. The
heroine of the opera appears and she meets his
requirements. He marries her and for a while
she seems blest. But the siren, the *Lola* in the case,
winds her toils about him as the disease stretches
him on the floor at her feet. Piquancy again,

achieved now without that poor palliative, punishment of the evil-doer.

Tasca's "A Santa Lucia" has an appetizing story
about an oysterman's son who deserts a woman by
whom he has a child, in order to marry one to whom
he had previously been affianced. The women
meet. There is a dainty brawl, and the fiancée of
Cicillo (he's the oysterman's son) strikes her rival's
child to the ground. The mother tries to stab the
fiancée with the operatic Italian woman's ever-
ready dagger, and this act stirs up the embers of
Cicillo's love. He takes the mother of his child back
home — to his father's house, that is. The child
must be some four years old by this time, but the
oysterman — dear, unsuspecting old man ! — knows
nothing about the relation existing between his son
and his housekeeper. He is thinking of marriage
with his common law daughter-in-law when in
comes the old fiancée with a tale for *Cicillo's* ears
of his mistress's unfaithfulness. "It is not true !"
shrieks the poor woman, but the wretch, her seducer,
closes his ears to her protestations ; and she throws
herself into the sea, where the oysters come from.
Cicillo rushes after her and bears her to the shore,
where she dies in his arms, gasping *in articulo mortis*,
"It is not true !"

*
* *

The romantic interest in Mascagni's life is confined to the period which preceded his sudden rise

to fame. His father was a baker in Leghorn, and there he was born on December 7, 1863. Of humble origin and occupation himself, the father, nevertheless, had large ambitions for his son; but not in the line of art. Pietro was to be shaped intellectually for the law. Like Handel, the boy studied the pianoforte by stealth in the attic. Grown in years, he began attending a music-school, when, it is said, his father confined him to his house; thence his uncle freed him and took over his care upon himself. Singularly enough, the man who at the height of his success posed as the most Italian of Italian masters had his inspiration first stirred by German poetry. Early in his career Beethoven resolved to set Schiller's "Hymn to Joy"; the purpose remained in his mind for forty years or so, and finally became a realization in the finale of the Ninth Symphony. Pietro Mascagni resolved as a boy to compose music for the same ode; and did it at once. Then he set to work upon a two-act opera, "Il Filanda." His uncle died, and a Count Florestan (here is another Beethovenian echo!) sent him to the Conservatory at Milan, where, like nearly all of his native contemporaries, he imbibed knowledge (and musical ideas) from Ponchielli.

After two years or so of academic study he yielded to a gypsy desire and set out on his wanderings, but not until he had chosen as a companion Maffei's translation of Heine's "Ratcliff" — a gloomy romance which seems to have caught the fancy of many composers. There followed five years of as checkered a life as ever musician led. Over and over again he was engaged as conductor of an itinerant or stationary operetta and opera company, only to have the enterprise fail and leave him stranded. For six weeks in Naples his daily ration was a plate of macaroni. But he worked at his opera steadily, although, as he once remarked, his dreams of fame were frequently swallowed up in the growls of his stomach, which caused him more trouble than many a millionaire suffers from too little appetite or too much gout. Finally, convinced that he could do better as a teacher of the pianoforte, he ran away from an engagement which paid him two dollars a day, and, sending off the manuscript of "Ratcliff" in a portmanteau, settled down in Cerignola. There he became director of a school for orchestral players, though he had first to learn to play the instruments; he also taught pianoforte and thoroughbass, and eked out a troublous existence until his success in competition for the prize offered by Sonzogno, the Milanese publisher, made him famous in a day and started him on the road to wealth.

It was but natural that, after "Cavalleria rusticana" had virulently affected the whole world with what the enemies of Signor Mascagni called "Mascagnitis," his next opera should be looked forward to with feverish anxiety. There was but a year to wait, for "L'Amico Fritz" was brought

forward in Rome on the last day of October, 1891.
Within ten weeks its title found a place on the programme of one of Mr. Walter Damrosch's Sunday
night concerts in New York; but the music was a
disappointment. Five numbers were sung by Mme.
Tavary and Signor Campanini, and Mr. Damrosch,
not having the orchestral parts, played the accom-
paniments upon a pianoforte. As usual, Mr. Gustav
Hinrichs was to the fore with a performance in
Philadelphia (on June 8, 1892), the principal singers
being Mme. Koert-Kronold, Clara Poole, M. Guille,
and Signor Del Puente. On January 31, 1893, the
Philadelphia singers, aided by the New York Symphony Society, gave a performance of the opera,
under the auspices of the Young Men's Hebrew
Association, for the benefit of its charities, at the
Carnegie Music Hall, New York. Mr. Walter
Damrosch was to have conducted, but was de-
tained in Washington by the funeral of Mr. Blaine,
and Mr. Hinrichs took his place. Another year
elapsed, and then, on January 10, 1894, the opera
reached the Metropolitan Opera House. In spite
of the fact that Madame Calvé sang the part
of *Suzel*, only two performances were given to the
work.

The failure of this opera did not dampen the
industry of Mascagni nor the zeal of his enterprising
publishers. For his next opera the composer went
again to the French authors, Erckmann-Chatrian,
who had supplied him with the story of "L'Amico

Fritz." This time he chose "Les deux Frères," which they had themselves turned into a drama with the title of "Rantzau." Mascagni's librettist retained the title. The opera came out in Florence in 1892. The tremendous personal popularity of the composer, who was now as much a favorite in Vienna and Berlin as he was in the town of his birth which had struck a medal in his honor, or the town of his residence which had created him an honorary citizen, could not save the work.

Now he turned to the opera which he had laid aside to take up his "Cavalleria," and in 1895 "Guglielmo Ratcliff," based upon the gloomy Scotch story told by Heine, was brought forward at La Scala, in Milan. It was in a sense the child of his penury and suffering, but he had taken it up inspired by tremendous enthusiasm for the subject, and inasmuch as most of its music had been written before success had turned his head, or desire for notoriety had begun to itch him, there was reason to hope to find in it some of the hot blood which surges through the score of "Cavalleria." As a matter of fact, critics who have seen the score or heard the work have pointed out that portions of "I Rantzau" and "Cavalleria" are as alike as two peas. It would not be a violent assumption that the composer in his eagerness to get his score before the Sonzogno jury had plucked his early work of its best feathers and found it difficult to restore

plumage of equal brilliancy when he attempted to
make restitution. In the same year, 1895, his next
opera, "Silvano," made a fiasco in Milan. A year
later there appeared "Zanetto," which seems like
an effort to contract the frame of the lyric drama
still further than is done in "Cavalleria." It is a
bozzetto, a sketch, based on Coppée's duologue "Le
Passant," a scene between a strumpet who is weary
of the world and a young minstrel. Its orchestration is unique — there are but strings and a harp. It
was brought out at Pesaro, where, in 1895, Mascagni
had been appointed director of the Liceo Musicale
Rossini.

As director of the music-school in Rossini's
native town Mascagni's days were full of trouble
from the outset. He was opposed, said his friends,
in reformatory efforts by some of the professors and
pupils, whose enmity grew so virulent that in 1897
they spread the story that he had killed himself.
He was deposed from his position by the administration, but reinstated by the Minister of Fine Arts.
The criticism followed him for years that he had
neglected his duties to travel about Europe, giving
concerts and conducting his operas for the greater
glory of himself and the profit of his publisher. At
the time of the suicide story it was also said that he
was in financial straits; to which his friends replied
that he received a salary of 60 lire ($12) a day as
director, 1000 lire ($200) a month from Sonzogno,
and lived in a princely dwelling.

After "Zanetto" came "Iris," to which, as the one opera besides "Cavalleria rusticana" which has remained in the American repertory, I shall devote the next chapter in this book. "Iris" was followed by "Le Maschere," which was brought out on January 17, 1901, simultaneously in six cities — Rome, Milan, Venice, Genoa, Turin, and Naples. It made an immediate failure in all of these places except Rome, where it endured but a short time. Mascagni's next operatic work was a lyric drama, entitled "Vistilia," the libretto of which, based upon an historical novel by Racco de Zerbi, was written by Menasci and Targioni-Tozzetti, who collaborated on the book of "Cavalleria rusticana." The action goes back to the time of Tiberius and deals with the loves of Vistilia and Helius. Then came another failure in the shape of "Amica," which lived out its life in Monte Carlo, where it was produced in March, 1905.

In the winter of 1902–1903 Signor Mascagni was in the United States for the purpose of conducting performances of some of his operas and giving concerts. The company of singers and instrumentalists which his American agents had assembled for his purpose was, with a few exceptions, composed of the usual operatic flotsam and jetsam which can be picked up at any time in New York. The enterprise began in failure and ended in scandal. There had been no adequate preparation for the operas announced, and one of them was not attempted.

This was "Ratcliff." "Cavalleria rusticana," "Zanetto," and "Iris" were poorly performed at the
Metropolitan Opera House in October, and an
attempt at Sunday night concerts was made.
Signor Mascagni's countrymen labored hard to
create enthusiasm for his cause, but the general
public remained indifferent. Having failed miser-
ably in New York, Mascagni, heavily burdened with
debt, went to Boston. There he was arrested for
breach of contract. He retaliated with a suit for
damages against his American managers. The
usual amount of crimination and recrimination followed, but eventually the difficulties were compounded and Mascagni went back to his home a
sadly disillusionized man.[1]

"Zanetto" was produced along with "Cavalleria
rusticana" at the Metropolitan Opera House on
October 8, 1902, and "Iris" on October 16. Signor
Mascagni conducted and the parts were distributed
as follows among the singers of the company:
Iris, Marie Farneti; *Osaka*, Pietro Schiavazzi;
Kyoto, Virgilio Bollati; *Il Cieco*, Francesco
Navarrini; *Una Guecha*, Dora de Filippe; *Un
Mercianola*, Pasquale Blasio; *Un Cencianola*, Ber-
nardino Landino. The opera was not heard of
again until the season of 1907-1908, when, just be-

---

[1] The story of this visit is told in greater detail in my "Chapters of Opera," as is also the story of the rivalry among American managers to be first in the field with "Cavalleria rusticana."

fore the end of the administration of Heinrich Conried, it was incorporated into the repertory of the Metropolitan Opera House apparently for the purpose of giving Mme. Emma Eames an opportunity to vie with Miss Geraldine Farrar in Japanese opera.

M

CHAPTER XI

"IRIS"

"LIGHT is the language of the eternal ones —
hear it!" proclaims the librettist of "Iris" in that
portion of his book which is neither said nor sung
nor played. And it is the sun that sings with
divers voices after the curtain has risen on a noc-
turnal scene, and the orchestra has sought to depict
the departure of the night, the break of day, the
revivification of the flowers and the sunrise. As
Byron sang of him, so Phœbus Apollo celebrates
himself as "the god of life and poetry and light,"
but does not stop there. He is also Infinite Beauty,
Cause, Reason, Poetry, and Love. The music begins with an all but inaudible descending passage in
the basses, answered by sweet concordant harmonies.
A calm song tells of the first streaks of light; wood-
wind and harp add their voices; a mellifluous hymn
chants the stirring flowers, and leads into a rhythmically, more incisive, but still sustained, orchestral
song, which bears upon its surface the choral proclamation of the sun: "I am! I am life! I am Beauty
infinite!" The flux and reflux of the instrumental
surge grows in intensity, the music begins to glow

162

with color and pulsate with eager life, and reaches
a mighty sonority, gorged with the crash of a
multitude of tamtams, cymbals, drums, and bells,
at the climacteric reiteration of *"Calore! Luce!
Amor!"* The piece is thrillingly effective, but as
little operatic as the tintinnabulatory chant of the
cherubim in the prologue of Boito's "Mefistofele."

And now allegory makes room for the drama.
To the door of her cottage, embowered on the banks
of a quiet stream, comes *Iris*. The peak of Fujiyama glows in the sunlight. *Iris* is fair and youthful and innocent. A dream has disturbed her.
"Gorgons and Hydras and Chimæras dire" had
filled her garden and threatened her doll, which she
had put to sleep under a rose-bush. But the sun's
rays burst forth and the monsters flee. She lifts
her doll and moves its arms in mimic salutation to
the sun. *Osaka*, a wealthy rake, and *Kyoto*, a
pander, play spy on her actions, gloat on her loveliness and plot to steal her and carry her to the
Yoshiwara. To this end they go to bring on a
puppet show, that its diversion may enable them to
steal her away without discovery. Women come
down to the banks of the river and sing pretty meta-
phors as they wash their basketloads of muslins.
Gradually the music of samisens, gongs, and drums
approaches. *Osaka* and *Kyoto* have disguised
themselves as travelling players, gathered together
some geishas and musicians, and now set up a
marionette theatre. *Iris* comforts her blind father,

the only object of her love, besides her doll, and promises to remain at his side. The puppet play tells the story of a maiden who suffers abuse from a cruel father, who threatens to sell her to a merchant. *Iris* is much affected by the sorrows of the puppet. The voice of Jor, the son of the sun, is heard — it is *Osaka*, singing without. The melody is the melody of *Turridu's* Siciliano, but the words are a promise of a blissful, kissful death and thereafter life everlasting. The puppet dies and with Jor dances off into Nirvana. Now three geishas, representing Beauty, Death, and the Vampire, begin a dance. *Kyoto* distracts the attention of the spectators while the dancers flaunt their skirts higher and wider until their folds conceal *Iris*, and *Osaka's* hirelings seize her and bear her off toward the city. *Kyoto* places a letter and money at the cottage door for the blind father. Through a pedler and the woman he learns that his daughter is gone to be an inmate of the Yoshiwara. He implores the people who had been jeering him to lead him thither, that he may spit in her face and curse her.

Iris is asleep upon a bed in the "Green House" of the district, which needs no description. A song, accompanied by the twanging of a samisen and the clanging of tamtams, is sung by three geishas. *Kyoto* brings in *Osaka* to admire her beauty, and sets a high price upon it. *Osaka* sends for jewels. *Iris* awakes and speculates in philosophical vein touch-

ing the question of her existence. She cannot be
dead, for death brings knowledge and paradise joy;
but she weeps. *Osaka* appears. He praises her
rapturously — her form, her hair, her eyes, her
mouth, her smile. *Iris* thinks him veritably Jor,
but he says his name is "Pleasure." The maiden
recoils in terror. A priest had taught her in an
allegory that Pleasure and Death were one! *Osaka*
loads her with jewels, fondles her, draws her to his
breast, kisses her passionately. *Iris* weeps. She
knows nothing of passion, and longs only for her
father, her cottage, and her garden. *Osaka* wearies
of his guest, but *Kyoto* plans to play still further
upon his lust. He clothes her in richer robes, but
more transparent, places her upon a balcony, and,
withdrawing a curtain, exhibits her beauty to the
multitude in the street. Amazed cries greet the
revelation. *Osaka* returns and pleads for her love.

"*Iris!*" It is the cry of the blind man hunting
the child whom he thinks has sold herself into disgraceful slavery. The crowd falls back before him,
while *Iris* rushes forward to the edge of the veranda
and cries out to him, that he may know her presence.
He gathers a handful of mud from the street and
hurls it in the direction of her voice. "There!
In your face! In your forehead! In your mouth!
In your eyes! *Fango!*" Under the imprecations
of her father the mind of *Iris* gives way. She
rushes along a corridor and hurls herself out of a
window.

The third act is reached, and drama merges again into allegory. In the wan light of the moon rag-pickers, men and women, are dragging their hooks through the slimy muck that flows through the open sewer beneath the fatal window. They sing mockingly to the moon. A flash of light from Fujiyama awakens a glimmer in the filth. Again. They rush forward and pull forth the body of *Iris* and begin to strip it of its adornments. She moves and they fly in superstitious fear. She recovers consciousness, and voices from invisible singers tell her of the selfish inspirations of *Osaka, Kyoto,* and her blind father; *Osaka's* desire baffled by fate — such is life! *Kyoto's* slavery to pleasure and a hangman's reward; — such is life! The blind man's dependence on his child for creature comforts; — such is life! *Iris* bemoans her fate as death comes gently to her. The sky grows rosy and the light brings momentary life. She stretches out her arms to the sun and acclaims the growing orb. As once upon Ida —

> Glad earth perceives and from her bosom pours
> Unbidden herbs and voluntary flow'rs !

A field of blossoms spreads around her, into which she sinks, while the sun, again many-voiced and articulate, chants his glory as in the beginning.

The story is perhaps prettier in the telling than in the performance. What there is in its symbolism and its poetical suggestion that is ingratiating is

more effective in the fancy than in the experience.
There are fewer clogs, fewer stagnant pools, fewer
eddies which whirl to no purpose. In the modern
school, with its distemper music put on in splotches,
there must be more merit and action. Psychological delineation in music which stimulates action,
or makes one forget the want of outward movement,
demands a different order of genius than that which
Signor Mascagni possesses. Mere talent for artful
device will not suffice. There are many effective
bits of expressive writing in the score of "Iris,"
but most of them are fugitive and aim at coloring a
word, a phrase, or at best a temporary situation.
There is little flow of natural, fervent melody.
What the composer accomplished with tune, characteristic but fluent, eloquent yet sustained, in
"Cavalleria rusticana," he tries to achieve in
"Iris" with violent, disjointed shifting of keys and
splashes of instrumental color. In this he is seldom successful, for he is not a master of orchestral
writing — that technical facility which nearly all
the young musicians have in the same degree that
all pianists have finger technic. His orchestral
stream is muddy; his effects generally crass and
empty of euphony. He throws the din of outlandish
instruments of percussion, a battery of gongs, big
and little, drums, and cymbals into his score without
achieving local color. Once only does he utilize
it so as to catch the ears and stir the fancy of his
listeners — in the beginning of the second act,

where there is a murmur of real Japanese melody. As a rule, however, Signor Mascagni seems to have been careless in the matter of local color, properly so, perhaps, for, strictly speaking, local color in the lyric drama is for comedy with its petty limitations, not for tragedy with its appeal to large and universal passions.   Yet it is in the lighter scenes, the scenes of comedy, like the marionette show, the scenes of mild pathos, like the monologues of *Iris*, and the scenes of mere accessory decoration, like that of the laundresses, the *mousmés* in the first act, with its purling figure borrowed from "Les Huguenots" and its unnecessarily uncanny col legno effect conveyed from "L'Africaine" that it is most effective.

CHAPTER XII

THIS is the book of the generation of "Madama Butterfly": An adventure in Japan begat Pierre Loti's "Madame Chrysanthème"; "Madame Chrysanthème" begat John Luther Long's "Madame Butterfly," a story; "Madame Butterfly," the story, begat "Madame Butterfly," a play by David Belasco; "Madame Butterfly," the play, begat "Madama Butterfly," the opera by Giacomo Puccini. The heroine of the roving French romanticist is therefore seen in her third incarnation in the heroine of the opera book which L. Illica and G. Giacosa made for Puccini. But in operatic essence she is still older, for, as Dr. Korngold, a Viennese critic, pointed out, *Selica* is her grandmother and *Lakmé* her cousin.

Even this does not exhaust her family history; there is something like a bar sinister in her escutcheon. Mr. Belasco's play was not so much begotten, conceived, or born of admiration for Mr. Long's book as it was of despair wrought by the failure of another play written by Mr. Belasco. This play was a farce entitled "Naughty Anthony," created by Mr. Belasco in a moment of æsthetic aberration

169

for production at the Herald Square Theatre, in
New York, in the spring of 1900. Mr. Belasco
doesn't think so now, but at the time he had a
notion that the public would find something humor-
ous and attractive in the spectacle of a popular
actress's leg swathed in several layers of stocking.
So he made a show of Blanche Bates. The public
refused to be amused at the farcical study in comparative anatomy, and when Mr. Belasco's friends
began to fault him for having pandered to a low
taste, and he felt the smart of failure in addition,
he grew heartily ashamed of himself. His affairs,
moreover, began to take on a desperate aspect;
the season threatened to be a ruinous failure, and
he had no play ready to substitute for "Naughty
Anthony." Some time before a friend had sent
him Mr. Long's book, but he had carelessly tossed
it aside. In his straits it came under his eyes
again, and this time he saw a play in it — a play
and a promise of financial salvation. It was late at
night when he read the story, but he had come to
a resolve by morning and in his mind's eye had already seen his actors in Japanese dress. The drama
lay in the book snugly enough; it was only necessary to dig it out and materialize it to the vision.
That occupation is one in which Mr. Belasco is at
home. The dialogue went to his actors a few pages
at a time, and the pictures rose rapidly in his mind.
Something different from a stockinged leg now !

Glimpses of Nippon — its mountains, waters,

bridges, flowers, gardens, geishas; as a foil to their
grace and color the prosaic figures of a naval officer
and an American Consul. All things tinged with
the bright light of day, the glories of sunset or the
super-glories of sunrise. We must saturate the
fancy of the audience with the atmosphere of
Japan, mused Mr. Belasco. Therefore, Japanese
scenes, my painter! Electrician, your plot shall
be worked out as carefully as the dialogue and action
of the play's people. "First drop discovered;
house-lights down; white foots with blue full work
change of color at back of drop; white lens on top
of mountain; open light with white, straw, amber,
and red on lower part of drop; when full on lower
footlights to blue," and so on. Mr. Belasco's
emotions, we know, find eloquent expression in
stage lights. But the ear must be carried off to the
land of enchantment as well as the eye. "Come,
William Furst, recall your experiences on the West-
ern coast. For my first curtain I want a quaint,
soft Japanese melody, *pp* — you know how !"

And so "Madame Butterfly," the play, was made.
In two weeks all was ready, and a day after the
first performance at the Herald Square Theatre,
on March 5, 1900, the city began to hum with eager
comment on the dramatic intensity of the scene of
a Japanese woman's vigil, of the enthralling eloquence of a motionless, voiceless figure, looking
steadily through a hole torn through a paper par-
tition, with a sleeping child and a nodding maid

at her feet, while a mimic night wore on, the lanterns on the floor flickered out one by one and the soft violins crooned a melody to the arpeggios of a harp.

The season at the Herald Square Theatre was saved. Some time later, when Mr. Belasco accompanied Mr. Charles Frohman to London to put on "Zaza" at the Garrick Theatre, he took "Madame Butterfly" with him and staged it at the Duke of York's Theatre, hard by. On the first night of "Madame Butterfly" Mr. Frohman was at the latter playhouse, Mr. Belasco at the former. The fall of the curtain on the little Japanese play was followed by a scene of enthusiasm which endured so long that Mr. Frohman had time to summon his colleague to take a curtain call. At a stroke the pathetic play had made its fortune in London, and, as it turned out, paved the way for a new and larger triumph for Mr. Long's story. The musical critics of the London newspapers came to the house and saw operatic possibilities in the drama. So did Mr. Francis Nielson, at the time Covent Garden's stage manager, who sent word of the discovery to Signor Puccini. The composer came from Milan, and realized on the spot that the successor of "Tosca" had been found. Signori Illica and Giacosa, librettists in ordinary to Ricordi & Co., took the work of making the opera book in hand. Signor Illica's fancy had roamed in the Land of Flowers before; he had written the libretto for Mascagni's "Iris." The ephemeral life of

Cho-Cho-San was over in a few months, but by that time "Madama Butterfly," glorified by music, had lifted her wings for a new flight in Milan.

It is an old story that many operas which are recognized as masterpieces later, fail to find appreciation or approval when they are first produced. "Madama Butterfly" made a fiasco when brought forward at La Scala on February 17, 1904.[1]

So complete was the fiasco that in his anxiety to withdraw the work Signor Puccini is said to have offered to reimburse the management of the theatre for the expenditures entailed by the production.

---

[1] At this *première* Campanini was the conductor and the cast was as follows: *Butterfly*, Storchio; *Suzuki*, Giaconia; *Pinkerton*, Zenatello; *Sharpless*, De Luca; *Goro*, Pini-Corsi; *Bonzo*, Venturini; *Yakuside*, Wulmann. At the first performance in London, on July 10, 1905, at Covent Garden, the cast was: *Butterfly*, Destinn; *Suzuki*, Lejeune; *Pinkerton*, Caruso; *Sharpless*, Scotti; *Goro*, Dufriche; *Bonzo*, Cotreuil; *Yakuside*, Rossi. Conductor, Campanini. After the revision it was produced at Brescia on May 28, 1904, with Zenatello, of the original cast, Kruscenisld as *Butterfly*, and Bellati as *Sharpless*. The first American performances were in the English version, made by Mrs. R. H. Elkin, by the Savage Opera Company, which came to the Garden Theatre, New York, after a trial season in Washington, on November 12, 1906. It had a run of nearly three months before it reached the Metropolitan Opera House, on February 11, 1907. Mr. Walter Rothwell conducted the English performance, in which there were several changes of casts, the original *Butterfly* being Elza Szamozy (a Hungarian singer); *Suzuki*, Harriet Behne; *Pinkerton*, Joseph F. Sheehan, and *Sharpless*, Winifred Goff. Arturo Vigna conducted the first Italian performance at the Metropolitan, with Geraldine Farrar as *Butterfly*, Louise Homer as *Suzuki*, Caruso as *Pinkerton*, Scotti as *Sharpless*, and Albert Reiss as *Goro*.

Failures of this kind are frequently inexplicable, but it is possible that the unconventional character of the story and the insensibility of the Italians to national musical color other than their own, had a great deal to do with it in this case. Whatever the cause, the popular attitude toward the opera was displayed in the manner peculiar to Italy, the discontented majority whistling, shrilling on house keys, grunting, roaring, bellowing, and laughing in the good old-fashioned manner which might be set down as possessed of some virtuous merit if reserved for obviously stupid creations.

"The Pall Mall Gazette" reported that at the time the composer told a friend that on this fateful first night he was shut up in a small room behind the scenes, where he could hear nothing of what was going on on the stage or in the audience-room. On a similar occasion, nearly a century before, when "The Barber of Seville" scored an equally monumental failure, Rossini, in the conductor's chair, faced the mob, shrugged his shoulders, and clapped his hands to show his contempt for his judges, then went home and composedly to bed. Puccini, though he could not see the discomfiture of his opera, was not permitted to remain in ignorance of it. His son and his friends brought him the news. His collaborator, Giacosa, rushed into the room with dishevelled hair and staring eyes, crying: "I have suffered the passion of death!" while Signorina Storchio burst into such a flood of tears and sobs that it was feared she would be ill. Puccini was cut to the heart, but he did not lose faith in the work. He had composed it in love and knew its potentialities. His faith found justification when he produced it in Brescia three months later and saw it start out at once on a triumphal tour of the European theatres. His work of revision was not a large or comprehensive one. He divided the second act into two acts, made some condensations to relieve the long strain, wrote a few measures of introduction for the final scene, but refused otherwise to change the music. His fine sense of the dramatic had told him correctly when he planned the work that there ought not to be a physical interruption of the pathetic vigil out of which Blanche Bates in New York and Evelyn Millard in London had made so powerful a scene, but he yielded to the compulsion of practical considerations, trying to save respect for his better judgment by refusing to call the final scene an act, though he permitted the fall of the curtain; but nothing can make good the loss entailed by the interruption. The mood of the play is admirably preserved in the music of the intermezzo, but the mood of the listeners is hopelessly dissipated with the fall of the curtain. When the scene of the vigil is again disclosed, the charm and the pathos have vanished, never to return. It is true that a rigid application of the law of unities would seem to forbid that a vigil of an entire night from eve

till morning be compressed into a few minutes;
but poetic license also has rights, and they could
have been pleaded with convincing eloquence by
music, with its marvellous capacity for publishing
the conflicting emotions of the waiting wife.

*

* *

His ship having been ordered to the Asiatic
station, *Benjamin Franklin Pinkerton*, Lieutenant
in the United States Navy, follows a custom (not
at all unusual among naval officers, if Pierre Loti
is to be believed) and for the summer sojourn in
Japan leases a Japanese wife. (The word "wife"
is a euphemism for housekeeper, companion, play-
fellow, mistress, what not.) This is done in a
manner involving little ceremony, as is known to
travellers and others familiar with the social customs
of Nippon, through a *nakodo*, a marriage broker
or matrimonial agent. M. Loti called his man
Kangourou; Mr. Long gave his the name of Goro.
That, however, and the character of the simple
proceeding before a registrar is immaterial. M.
Loti, who assures us that his book is merely some
pages from a veritable diary, entertains us with
some details preliminary to his launch into a singular
kind of domestic existence, which are interesting as
bearing on the morals of the opera and as indicative
of the fact that he is a closer observer of Oriental
life than his American confrère. He lets us see

how merchantable "wives" are chosen, permits
M. Kangourou to exhibit his wares and expatiate
on their merits.   There is the daughter of a wealthy
China merchant, a young woman of great accomplishments who can write "commercially" and has
won a prize in a poetic contest with a sonnet.   She
is, consequently, very dear — 100 *yen*, say $100 —
but that is of no consequence; what matters is
that she has a disfiguring scar on her cheek.   She
will not do.   Then there is Mlle. Jasmin, a pretty
girl of fifteen years, who can be had for $18 or $20
a month (contract cancellable at the end of any
month for non-payment), a few dresses of fashion-
able cut and a pleasant house to live in.   Mlle.
Jasmin comes to be inspected with one old lady,
two old ladies, three old ladies (mamma and aunts),
and a dozen friends and neighbors, big and little.
Loti's moral stomach revolts at the thought of
buying for his uses a child who looks like a doll,
and is shocked at the public parade which has
been made of her as a commodity.   He has not yet
been initiated into some of the extraordinary customs of Japan, nor yet into some of the distinctions
attendant upon those customs.   He learns of one
of the latter when he suggests to the broker that
he might marry a charming geisha who had taken
his fancy at a tea house.   The manner in which
the suggestion was received convinced him that he
might as well have purposed to marry the devil
himself as a professional dancer and singer.   Among

N

the train of Mlle. Jasmin's friends is one less young than Mlle. Jasmin, say about eighteen, and already more of a woman; and when Loti says, "Why not her?" M. Kangourou trots her out for inspection and, discreetly sending Loti away, concludes the arrangement between night-fall and 10 o'clock, when he comes with the announcement: "All is arranged, sir; her parents will give her up for $20 a month — the same price as Mlle. Jasmin."

So Mlle. Chrysanthème became the wife of Pierre Loti during his stay at Nagasaki, and then dutifully went home to her mother without breaking her heart at all. But she was not a geisha, only a mousmé — "one of the prettiest words in the Nipponese language," comments M. Loti, "it seems almost as if there must be a little moue in the very sound, as if a pretty, taking little pout, such as they put on, and also a little pert physiognomy, were described by it."

Lieutenant Pinkerton, equally ignorant with Lieutenant Loti but uninstructed evidently, marries a geisha whose father had made the happy dispatch at the request of the Son of Heaven after making a blunder in his military command. She is Cio-Cio-San, also Madama Butterfly, and she comes to her wedding with a bevy of geishas or mousmés (I do not know which) and a retinue of relations. All enjoy the hospitality of the American officer while picking him to pieces, but turn from their kinswoman when they learn from an uncle, who is a

Buddhist priest and comes late to the wedding like
the wicked fairy in the stories, that she has attended
the Mission school and changed her religion.   Wherefore the *bonze* curses her: "Hou, hou ! *Cio-Cio-San,*
hou, hou ! "

Sharpless, United States Consul at Nagasaki, had
not approved of *Pinkerton's* adventure, fearing that
it might bring unhappiness to the little woman;
but *Pinkerton* had laughed at his scruples and
emptied his glass to the marriage with an American
wife which he hoped to make some day.   Neither
Loti nor Long troubles us with the details of so
prosaic a thing as the marriage ceremony; but
Puccini and his librettists make much of it, for it
provides the only opportunity for a chorus and the
musician had found delightfully mellifluous Japanese
gongs to add a pretty touch of local color to the
music.   *Cio-Cio-San* has been "outcasted" and
Pinkerton comforts her and they make love in the
starlight (after *Butterfly* has changed her habili-
ments) like any pair of lovers in Italy.   "Dolce
notté ! Quante stelle ! Vieni, vieni !" for quantity.

This is the first act of the opera, and it is all
expository to Belasco's "Tragedy of Japan," which
plays in one act, with the pathetic vigil separating
the two days which form its period of action.   When
that, like the second act of the opera, opens, *Pinkerton* has been gone from Nagasaki and his "wife"
three years, and a baby boy of whom he has never
heard, but who has his eyes and hair has come to

bear *Butterfly* company in the little house on the hill. The money left by the male butterfly when he flitted is all but exhausted. *Madama Butterfly* appears to be lamentably ignorant of the customs of her country, for she believes herself to be a wife in the American sense and is fearfully wroth with *Suzuki*, her maid, when she hints that she never knew a foreign husband to come back to a Japanese wife. But *Pinkerton* when he sailed away had said that he would be back "when the robins nest again," and that suffices *Cio-Cio-San*. But when *Sharpless* comes with a letter to break the news that his friend is coming back with an American wife, he loses courage to perform his mission at the contemplation of the little woman's faith in the truant. Does he know when the robins nest in America? In Japan they had nested three times since *Pinkerton* went away. The consul quails at that and damns his friend as a scoundrel. Now *Goro*, who knows *Butterfly's* pecuniary plight, brings *Yamadori* to her. *Yamadori* is a wealthy Japanese citizen of New York in the book and play and a prince in the opera, but in all he is smitten with *Butterfly's* beauty and wants to add her name to the list of wives he has conveniently married and as conveniently divorced on his visits to his native land. *Butterfly* insists that she is an American and cannot be divorced Japanese fashion, and is amazed when *Sharpless* hints that *Pinkerton* might have forgotten her and she would better accept *Yamadori's* hand.

First she orders him out of the house, but, repenting her of her rudeness, brings in the child to show him something that no one is likely to forget. She asks the consul to write to his friend and tell him that he has a son, so fine a son, indeed, that she indulges in a day dream of the Mikado stopping at the head of his troops to admire him and make him a prince of the realm. *Sharpless* goes away with his mission unfulfilled and *Suzuki* comes in dragging *Goro* with her, for that he had been spreading scandalous tales about the treatment which children born like this child receive in America. *Butterfly* is tempted to kill the wretch, but at the last is content to spurn him with her foot.

At this moment a cannon shot is heard. A man-of-war is entering the harbor. Quick, the glasses! "Steady my hand, *Suzuki*, that I may read the name." It is the Abraham Lincoln, *Pinkerton's* ship! Now the cherry tree must give up its every blossom, every bush or vine its violets and jessamines to garnish the room for his welcome! The garden is stripped bare, vases are filled, the floor is strewn with petals. Perfumes exhale from the voices of the women and the song of the orchestra. Here local color loses its right; the music is all Occidental. *Butterfly* is dressed again in her wedding gown of white and her pale cheeks are touched up with carmine. The paper partitions are drawn against the night. *Butterfly* punctures the *shoji* with three holes — one high up for herself

to look through, standing; one lower for the maid
to look through, sitting; one near the floor for the
baby. And so *Butterfly* stands in an all-night vigil.
The lanterns flicker and go out. Maid and babe
sink down in sleep. The gray dawn creeps over
the waters of the harbor. Human voices, transformed into instruments, hum a barcarolle. (We
heard it when *Sharpless* tried to read the letter.)
A Japanese tune rises like a sailors' chanty from
the band. Mariners chant their "Yo ho!" Day
is come. *Suzuki* awakes and begs her mistress to
seek rest. *Butterfly* puts the baby to bed, singing
a lullaby. *Sharpless* and *Pinkerton* come and
learn of the vigil from *Suzuki*, who sees the form
of a lady in the garden and hears that it is the
American wife of *Pinkerton*. *Pinkerton* pours out
his remorse melodiously. He will be haunted forever by the picture of his once happy home and
Cio-Cio-San's reproachful eyes. He leaves money
for *Butterfly* in the consul's hands and runs away
like a coward. *Kate*, the American wife, and
Suzuki meet in the garden. The maid is asked
to tell her mistress the meaning of the visit, but
before she can do so *Butterfly* sees them. Her questions bring out half the truth; her intuition tells
her the rest. *Kate* (an awful blot she is on the
dramatic picture) begs forgiveness and asks for the
baby boy that her husband may rear him. *Butterfly*
says he shall have him in half an hour if he will
come to fetch him. She goes to the shrine of

Buddha and takes from it a veil and a dagger,
reading the words engraved on its blade: "To
die with honor when one can no longer live with
honor." It is the weapon which the Mikado had
sent to her father. She points the weapon at her
throat, but at the moment *Suzuki* pushes the baby
into the room. *Butterfly* addresses it passionately;
then, telling it to play, seats it upon a stool, puts
an American flag into its hands, a bandage around
its eyes. Again she takes dagger and veil and
goes behind a screen. The dagger is heard to fall.
Butterfly totters out from behind the screen with a
veil wound round her neck. She staggers to the
child and falls, dying, at its feet. *Pinkerton* rushes
in with a cry of horror and falls on his knees, while
Sharpless gently takes up the child.

*
* *

I have no desire to comment disparagingly upon
the *dénouement* of the book of Mr. Long or the play
of Mr. Belasco which Puccini and his librettists
followed; but in view of the origin of the play a
bit of comparative criticism seems to be imperative.
Loti's "Madame Chrysanthème" was turned into
an opera by André Messager. What the opera
was like I do not know. It came, it went, and
left no sign; yet it would seem to be easy to guess
at the reason for its quick evanishment. If it
followed the French story, as no doubt it did, it

was too faithful to the actualities of Japanese life
to awaken a throb of emotion in the Occidental
heart. Without such a throb a drama is naught
— a sounding brass and tinkling cymbal. The
charm of Loti's book lies in its marvellously beautiful portrayal of a country, a people, and a characteristic incident in the social life of that people.
Its interest as a story, outside of the charm of its
telling, is like that excited by inspection of an
exotic curio. In his dedication of the book the
author begged Mme. la Duchesse de Richelieu not
to look for any meaning in it, but to receive it in
the same spirit in which she would receive "some
quaint bit of pottery, some grotesque carved ivory
idol, or some preposterous trifle brought back from
the fatherland of all preposterousness." It is a
record of a bit of the wandering life of a poet who
makes himself a part of every scene into which
fortune throws him. He has spent a summer with
a Japanese *mousmé*, whom he had married Japanese
fashion, and when he has divorced her, also in
Japanese fashion, with regard for all the conven-
tions, and sailed away from her forever, he is more
troubled by thoughts of possible contamination to
his own nature than because of any consequences
to the woman. Before the final farewell he had
felt a touch of pity for the "poor little gypsy,"
but when he mounted the stairs to her room for
the last time he heard her singing, and mingled
with her voice was a strange metallic sound, *dzinn,*

drinn! as of coins ringing on the floor. Is she
amusing herself with quoits, or the *jeu du crapaud,*
or pitch and toss? He creeps in, and there, dressed
for the departure to her mother's, sitting on the
floor is Chrysanthème; and spread out around
her all the fine silver dollars he had given her according to agreement the night before. "With
the competent dexterity of an old money changer
she fingers them, turns them over, throws them
on the floor, and armed with a little mallet *ad hoc,*
rings them vigorously against her ear, singing the
while I know not what little pensive, birdlike song,
which I dare say she improvises as she goes along.
Well, after all, it is even more completely Japanese
than I could possibly have imagined it — this last
scene of my married life! I feel inclined to laugh."
And he commends the little gypsy's worldly wisdom,
offers to make good any counterfeit piece which she
may find, and refuses to permit her to see him go
aboard of his ship. She does, nevertheless, along
with the Japanese wives of four of his fellow officers,
who peep at their flitting husbands through the cur-
tains of their sampans. But when he is far out on
the great Yellow Sea he throws the faded lotus
flowers which she had given him through the port-
hole of his cabin, making his best excuses for "giving
to them, natives of Japan, a grave so solemn and
so vast"; and he utters a prayer: "O Ama-Térace-
Omi-Kami, wash me clean from this little marriage
of mine in the waters of the river of Kamo!"

The story has no soul, and to give his story, which borrowed its motive from Loti's, a soul, Mr. Long had to do violence to the verities of Japanese life. Yet might not even a geisha feel a genuine passion?

*
* *

The use of folk-tunes in opera is older than "Madama Butterfly," but Puccini's score stands alone in the extent of the use and the consistency with which Japanese melody has been made the foundation of the music. When Signor Illica, one of the librettists, followed Sâr Péladan and d'Annunzio into Nippon seeking flowers for "Iris," he took Mascagni with him — metaphorically, of course. But Mascagni was a timid gleaner. Puccini plucked with a bolder hand, as indeed he might, for he is an incomparably greater adept in the art of making musical nosegays. In fact, I know of only one score that is comparable with that of "Madama Butterfly" in respect of its use of national musical color, and that is "Boris Godounoff." Moussorgsky, however, had more, richer, and a greater variety of material to work with than Puccini. Japanese music is arid and angular, and yet so great is Puccini's skill in combining creative imagination and reflection that he knew how to make it blossom like a rose. Pity that he could not wholly overcome its rhythmical monotony. Japanese melody runs almost uninterruptedly through his instrumental score, giving way at intervals to the Italian style of lyricism when the characters and passions become universal rather than local types. Structurally, his score rests on the Wagnerian method, in that the vocal part floats on an uninterrupted instrumental current. In the orchestral part the tunes which he borrowed from the popular music of Japan are continuously recurrent, and fragments of them are used as the connecting links of the whole fabric. He uses also a few typical themes (*Leitmotive*) of his own invention, and to them it might be possible, by ingenious study of their relation to text and situation, to attach significances in the manner of the Wagnerian handbooks; but I do not think that such processes occupied the composer's mind to any considerable extent, and the themes are not appreciably characteristic. His most persistent use of a connecting link, arbitrarily chosen, is found in the case of the first motive of the theme, which he treats fugally in the introduction, and which appears thereafter to the end of the chapter (*a*, in the list of themes printed herewith). What might be called personal themes are the opening notes of "The Star-Spangled Banner" for *Pinkerton* and the melody (*d*) which comes in with *Yamadori*, in which the Japanese tune used by Sir Arthur Sullivan in "The Mikado" is echoed. The former fares badly throughout the score (for which no blame need attach to Signor Puccini), but the latter is used with capital effect, though not always in connection with the character.

If Signor Puccini had needed the suggestion that Japanese music was necessary for a Japanese play (which of course he did not), he might have received it when he saw Mr. Belasco's play in London. For the incidental music in that play Mr. William Furst provided Japanese tunes, or tunes made over the very convenient Japanese last. Through Mr. Belasco's courtesy I am able to present here a relic of this original "Butterfly" music. The first melody (a) was the theme of the curtain-music; (b) that accompanying *Cho-Cho-San*, when discovered at the beginning spraying flowers, presenting an offering at the shrine and burning incense in the house at the foot of Higashi hill; (c) the *Yamadori* music; (d) the music accompanying the first production of the sword; (e) the music of the vigil. There were also two Occidental pieces — the melody of a little song which *Pinkerton* had taught *Cho-Cho-San*, "I Call Her the Belle of Japan," and "Rock-a-bye, Baby."

Themes from Puccini's "Butterfly" music
By permission of Ricordi & Co.

Melodies from Mr. Furst's "Butterfly" music
By permission of Mr. David Belasco

CHAPTER XIII

In the beginning there was "Guntram," of which we in America heard only fragmentary echoes in our concert-rooms. Then came "Feuersnot," which reached us in the same way, but between which and the subject which is to occupy me in this chapter there is a kinship through a single instrumental number, the meaning of which no commentator has dared more than hint at. It is the music which accompanies the episode, politely termed a "love scene," which occurs at the climax of the earlier opera, but is supposed to take place before the opening of the curtain in the later. Perhaps I shall recur to them again — if I have the courage.

These were the operas of Richard Strauss which no manager deemed it necessary or advisable to produce in New York. Now came "Salome." Popular neurasthenia was growing. Oscar Wilde thought France might accept a glorification of necrophilism and wrote his delectable book in French. France would have none of it, but when it was done into German, and Richard Strauss accentuated its sexual perversity by his hysterical music, lo! Berlin ac-

190

cepted it with avidity. The theatres of the Prussian capital were keeping pace with the pathological spirit of the day, and were far ahead of those of Paris, where, it had long been the habit to think, moral obliquity made its residence. If Berlin, then why not New York? So thought Mr. Conried, saturated with German theatricalism, and seeing no likely difference in the appeal of a "Parsifal," which he had successfully produced, and a "Salome," he prepared to put the works of Wagner and Strauss on the same footing at the Metropolitan Opera House. An influence which has not yet been clearly defined, but which did not spring from the director of the opera nor the gentlemen who were his financial backers, silenced the maunderings of the lust-crazed *Herod* and paralyzed the contortions of the lascivious dancer to whom he was willing to give one-half his kingdom.[1]

Now Mr. Hammerstein came to continue the artistic education which the owners of the Metropolitan Opera House had so strangely and unaccountably checked. *Salome* lived out her mad life in a short time, dying, not by the command of *Herod*, but crushed under the shield of popular opinion. The operation, though effective, was not as swift as it might have been had operatic conditions been different than they are in New York, and before it was accomplished a newer phase of Strauss's pathological

---

[1] For the story of "Salome" in New York, see my "Chapters of Opera" (Henry Holt & Co., New York), p. 343 *et seq.*

art had offered itself as a nervous excitation. It was "Elektra," and under the guise of an ancient religious ideal, awful but pathetic, the people were asked to find artistic delight in the contemplation of a woman's maniacal thirst for a mother's blood. It is not necessary to recall the history of the opera at the Manhattan Opera House to show that the artistic sanity of New York was proof against the new poison.

Hugo von Hoffmannsthal had aided Strauss in this brew and collaborated with him in the next, which, it was hoped, probably because of the difference in its concoction and ingredients, would make his rein even more taut than it had ever been on theatrical managers and their public. From the Greek classics he turned to the comedy of the Beaumarchais period. Putting their heads together, the two wrote "Der Rosenkavalier." It was perhaps shrewd on their part that they avoided all allusion to the *opera buffa* of the period and called their work a "comedy for music." It enabled them, in the presence of the ignorant, to assume a virtue which they did not possess; but it is questionable if that circumstance will help them any. It is only the curious critic nowadays who takes the trouble to look at the definition, or epithet, on a title page. It is the work which puts the hallmark on itself; not the whim of the composer. It would have been wise, very wise indeed, had Hoffmannsthal avoided everything which might call up a comparison between himself and Beaumarchais. It was simply fatal to Strauss that he tried to avoid all comparison between his treatment of an eighteenth century comedy and Mozart's. One of his devices was to make use of the system of musical symbols which are irrevocably associated with Wagner's method of composition. Mozart knew nothing of this system, but he had a better one in his Beaumarchaisian comedy, which "Der Rosenkavalier" recalls; it was that of thematic expression for each new turn in the dramatic situation — a system which is carried out so brilliantly in "Le Nozze di Figaro" that there is nothing, even in "Die Meistersinger," which can hold a candle to it. Another was to build up the vocal part of his comedy on orchestral waltzes. Evidently it was his notion that at the time of Maria Theresa (in whose early reign the opera is supposed to take place) the Viennese world was given over to the dance. It was so given over a generation later, so completely, indeed, that at the meetings in the ridotto, for which Mozart, Haydn, Gyrowetz, Beethoven, and others wrote music, retiring rooms had to be provided for ladies who were as unprepared for possible accidents as was one of those described by Pepys as figuring in a court ball in his time; but to put scarcely anything but waltz tunes under the dialogue of "Der Rosenkavalier" is an anachronism which is just as disturbing to the judicious as the fact that Herr Strauss, though he starts his half-dozen or more of waltzes most insinuatingly, never lets them run the natural course which Lanner and the Viennese

o

Strauss, who suggested their tunes, would have made them do.   Always, the path which sets out so prettily becomes a byway beset with dissonant thorns and thistles and clogged with rocks.

All of this is by way of saying that "Der Rosen-kavalier" reached New York on December 9, 1913, after having endured two years or so in Europe, under the management of Mr. Gatti-Casazza, and was treated with the distinction which Mr. Conried gave "Parsifal" and had planned for "Salome."   It was set apart for a performance outside the subscription, special prices were demanded, and the novelty dressed as sumptuously and prepared with as lavish an expenditure of money and care as if it were a work of the very highest importance.   Is it that? The question is not answered by the fact that its music was composed by Richard Strauss, even though one be willing to admit that Strauss is the greatest living master of technique in musical composition, the one concerning whose doings the greatest curiosity is felt and certainly the one whose doings are the best advertised.   "Der Rosenkavalier," in spite of all these things, must stand on its merits — as a comedy with music.   The author of its book has invited a comparison which has already been suggested by making it a comedy of intrigue merely and placing its time of action in Vienna and the middle of the eighteenth century.   He has gone further; he has invoked the spirit of Beaumarchais to animate his people and his incidents.   The one

thing which he could not do, or did not do, was to
supply the satirical scourge which justified the Figaro
comedies of his great French prototype and which,
while it made their acceptance tardy, because of
royal and courtly opposition, made their popular
triumph the more emphatic. "Le Nozze di Figaro"
gave us more than one figure and more than one
scene in the representation, and "Le Nozze di
Figaro" is to those who understand its text one of
the most questionable operas on the current list.
But there is a moral purpose underlying the comedy
which to some extent justifies its frank salaciousness.
It is to prevent the *Count* from exercising an ancient
seigniorial right over the heroine which he had volun-
tarily resigned, that all the characters in the play
unite in the intrigue which makes up the comedy.
Moreover, there are glimpses over and over again
of honest and virtuous love between the characters
and beautiful expressions of it in the music which
makes the play delightful, despite its salaciousness.
Even *Cherubino*, who seems to have come to life
again in *Octavian*, is a lovable youth if for no other
reason than that he represents youth in its amorous-
ness toward all womankind, with thought of special
mischief toward none.

"Der Rosenkavalier" is a comedy of lubricity
merely, with what little satirical scourge it has applied only to an old roué who is no more deserving
of it than most of the other people in the play. So
much of its story as will bear telling can be told very

briefly. It begins, assuming its instrumental introduction (played with the scene discreetly hidden)
to be a part of it, with a young nobleman locked in
the embraces of the middle-aged wife of a field
marshal, who is conveniently absent on a hunting
expedition. The music is of a passionate order, and
the composer, seeking a little the odor of virtue, but
with an oracular wink in his eye, says in a descriptive note that it is to be played in the spirit of parody
(*parodistisch*). Unfortunately the audience cannot
see the printed direction, and there is no parody in
music except extravagance and ineptitude in the
utterance of simple things (like the faulty notes of
the horns in Mozart's joke on the village musicians,
the cadenza for violin solo in the same musical joke,
or the twangling of *Beckmesser's* lute) ; so the introduction is an honest musical description of things
which the composer is not willing to confess, and
least of all the stage manager, for when the curtain
opens there is not presented even the picture called
for by the German libretto. Nevertheless, morn is
dawning, birds are twittering, and the young lover,
kneeling before his mistress on a divan, is bemoaning
the fact that day is come and that he cannot pub-
lish his happiness to the world. The tête-à-tête is
interrupted by a rude boor of a nobleman, who comes
to consult his cousin (the princess) about a messenger to send with the conventional offering of a silver
rose to the daughter of a vulgar plebeian just ele-
vated to the nobility because of his wealth. The

conversation between the two touches on little more than old amours, and after the lady has held her levee designed to introduce a variety of comedy effects in music as well as action, the princess recommends her lover for the office of rosebearer. Meanwhile the lover has donned the garments of a waiting maid and been overwhelmed with the wicked attentions of the roué, *Lerchenau*. When the lovers are again alone there is a confession of renunciation on the part of the princess, based on the philosophical reflection that, after all, her *Octavian* being so young would bring about the inevitable parting sooner or later.

In the second act what the princess in her prescient abnegation had foreseen takes place. Her lover carries the rose to the young woman whom the roué had picked out for his bride and promptly falls in love with her. She with equal promptness, following the example of Wagner's heroines, bowls herself at his head. The noble vulgarian complicates matters by insisting that he receive a dowry instead of paying one. The young hot-blood adds to the difficulties by pinking him in the arm with his sword, but restores order at the last by sending him a letter of assignation in his first act guise of a maid servant of the princess.

This assignation is the background of the third act, which is farce of the wildest and most vulgar order. Much of it is too silly for description. Always, however, there is allusion to the purpose of the meeting on the part of *Lerchenau*, whose plans are spoiled by apparitions in all parts of the room, the entrance of the police, his presumptive bride and her father, a woman who claims him as her husband, four children who raise bedlam (and memories of the contentious Jews in "Salome"), by shouting "Papa! papa!" until his mind is in a whirl and he rushes out in despair. The princess leaves the new-found lovers alone.

They hymn their happiness in Mozartian strains (the melody copied from the second part of the music with which *Papageno* sets the blackamoors to dancing in "Die Zauberflöte"), the orchestra talks of the matronly renunciation of the princess, enthusiastic Straussians of a musical parallel with the quintet from Wagner's "Meistersinger," and the opera comes to an end after three and one-half hours of more or less unintelligible dialogue poised on waltz melodies.

I have said unintelligible dialogue. For this unintelligibility there are two reasons — the chief one musical, the other literary. Though Strauss treats his voices with more consideration in "Der Rosenkavalier" than in his tragedies, he still so overburdens them that the words are distinguishable only at intervals. Only too frequently he crushes them with orchestral voices, which in themselves are not overwhelming — the voices of his horns, for instance, for which he shows a particular partiality. His style of declamation is melodic, though it is only at the end of the opera that he rises to real vocal melody; but it seems to be put over an orchestral part, and not the orchestral part put under it. There is no moment in which he can say, as Wagner truthfully and admiringly said of the wonderful orchestral music of the third act of "Tristan und Isolde," that all this swelling instrumental song existed only for the sake of what the dying *Tristan* was saying upon his couch. All of Strauss's waltzes seem to exist for their own sake, which makes the disappointment greater that they are not carried through in the spirit in which they are begun; that is, the spirit of the naïve Viennese dance tune.

A second reason for the too frequent unintelligibility of the text is its archaic character. Its idioms are eighteenth century as well as Viennese, and its persistent use of the third person even among individuals of quality, though it gives a tang to the libretto when read in the study, is not welcome when heard with difficulty. Besides this, there is use of dialect — vulgar when assumed by *Octavian*, mixed when called for by such characters as *Valzacchi* and his partner in scandal mongery, *Annina*. To be compelled to forego a knowledge of half of what such a master of diction as Mr. Reiss was saying was a new sensation to his admirers who understand German. Yet the fault was as little his as it was Mr. Goritz's that so much of what he said went for nothing; it was all his misfortune, including the fact that much of the music is not adapted to his voice.

The music offers a pleasanter topic than the

action and dialogue. It is a relief to those listeners who go to the opera oppressed with memories of "Salome" and "Elektra." It is not only that their ears are not so often assaulted by rude sounds, they are frequently moved by phrases of great and genuine beauty. Unfortunately the Straussian system of composition demands that beauty be looked for in fragments. Continuity of melodic flow is impossible to Strauss — a confession of his inability either to continue Wagner's method, to improve on it, or invent anything new in its place. The best that has been done in the Wagnerian line belongs to Humperdinck.[1]

[1] "Der Rosenkavalier" had its first American production at the Metropolitan Opera House, New York, on December 9, 1913, the cast being as follows:—

Feldmarschallin Fürstin Werdenberg	Frieda Hempel
Baron Ochs auf Lerchenau	Otto Goritz
Octavian, genannt Quinquin	Margarete Ober
Herr von Faninal	Hermann Weil
Sophie, seine Tochter	Anna Case
Jungfer Marianne Leitmetzerin	Rita Fornia
Valzacchi, ein Intrigant	Albert Reiss
Annina, seine Begleiterin	Marie Mattfeld
Ein Polizeikommissär	Carl Schlegel
Haushofmeister der Feldmarschallin	Pietro Audisio
Haushofmeister bei Faninal	Lambert Murphy
Ein Notar	Basil Ruysdael
Ein Wirt	Julius Bayer
Ein Sänger	Carl Jorn
Drei adelige Waisen	Louise Cox Rosina Van Dyck Sophie Braslau
Eine Modistin	Jeanne Maubourg
Ein Lakai	Ludwig Burgstaller
Ein kleiner Neger	Ruth Weinstein

Conductor — Alfred Hertz

CHAPTER XIV

"KÖNIGSKINDER"

ONCE upon a time a witch cast a spell upon a king's daughter and held her in servitude as a goose-herd. A prince found her in the forest and loved her. She loved him in return, and would gladly have gone away from her sordid surroundings with him, though she had spurned the crown which he had offered her in exchange for her wreath of flowers; but when she escaped from her jailer she found that she could not break the charm which held her imprisoned in the forest. Then the prince left the crown lying at her feet and continued his wanderings. Scarcely had he gone when there came to the hut of the witch a broommaker and a woodchopper, guided by a wandering minstrel. They were ambassadors from the city of Hellabrunn, which had been so long without a king that its boorish burghers themselves felt the need of a ruler in spite of their boorishness. To the wise woman the ambassadors put the questions: Who shall be this ruler and by what sign shall they recognize him? The witch tells them that their sovereign shall be the first person who enters their gates after the bells have rung the noon hour on the

201

morrow, which is the day of the Hella festival. Then the minstrel catches sight of the lovely goose-girl, and through the prophetic gift possessed by poets he recognizes in her a rightly born princess for his people. By the power of his art he is enabled to put aside the threatening spells of the witch and compel the hag to deliver the maiden into his care. He persuades her to break the enchantment which had held her bound hitherto and defy the wicked power.

Meanwhile, however, grievous misfortunes have befallen the prince, her lover. He has gone to Hella-brunn, and desiring to learn to serve in order that he might better know how to rule, he had taken service as a swineherd. The daughter of the innkeeper becomes enamoured of the shapely body of the prince, whose proud spirit she cannot understand, and who has repulsed her advances. His thoughts go back to the goosegirl whose wreath, with its fresh fragrance, reminds him of his duty. He attempts to teach the burghers their own worth, but the wench whose love he had repulsed accuses him of theft, and he is about to be led off to prison when the bells peal forth the festal hour.

Joyfully the watchmen throw open the strong town gates and the multitude and gathered councillors fall back to receive their king. But through the doors enters the gooseherd, proudly wearing her crown and followed by her flock and the minstrel. The lovers fall into each other's arms, but only the poet and a little child recognize them as of royal

blood. The boorish citizens, who had fancied that
their king would appear in regal splendor, drive the
youth and maiden out with contumely, burn the
witch and cripple the minstrel by breaking one of
his legs on the wheel. Seeking his home, the prince
and his love lose their way in the forest during a
snowstorm and die of a poisoned loaf made by the
witch, for which the prince had bartered his broken
crown, under the same tree which had sheltered
them on their first meeting; but the children of
Hellabrunn, who had come out in search of them,
guided by a bird, find their bodies buried under the
snow and give them royal acclaim and burial.
And the prescient minstrel hymns their virtues.

This is the story of Engelbert Humperdinck's opera
"Königskinder," which had its first performance on
any stage at the Metropolitan Opera House, New
York, on December 28, 1910, with the following cast:

Der Königssohn.................Herman Jadlowker
Die Gänsemagd....................Geraldine Farrar
Der Spielmann........................Otto Goritz
Die Hexe............................Louise Homer
Der Holzhacker.....................Adamo Didur
Der Besenbinder....................Albert Reiss
Zwei Kinder...........Edna Walter and Lotte Engel
Der Ratsälteste.....................Marcel Reiner
Der Wirt.......................Antonio Pini-Corsi
Die Wirtstochter.................Florence Wickham
Der Schneider.......................Julius Bayer
Die Stallmagd.....................Marie Mattfeld
Zwei Torwächter.....Ernst Maran and William Hinshaw
Conductor: Alfred Hertz

To some in the audience the drama was new only in the new operatic dress with which Humperdinck had clothed it largely at the instance of the Metropolitan management. It had been known as a spoken play for twelve years and three of its musical numbers — the overture and two pieces of between-acts music — had been in local concert-lists for the same length of time. The play had been presented with incidental music for many of the scenes as well as the overture and *entr'actes* in 1898 in an extremely interesting production at the Irving Place Theatre, then under the direction of Heinrich Conried, in which Agnes Sorma and Rudolf Christians had carried the principal parts. It came back four years later in an English version at the Herald Square Theatre, but neither in the German nor the English performance was it vouchsafed us to realize what had been the purpose of the author of the play and the composer of the music.

The author, who calls herself Ernst Rosmer, is a woman, daughter of Heinrich Porges, for many years a factotum at the Bayreuth festivals. It was her father's devotion to Wagner which gave her the name of Elsa. She married a lawyer and littérateur in Munich named Bernstein, and has written a number of plays besides "Königskinder," which she published in 1895, and afterward asked Herr Humperdinck (not yet a royal Prussian professor, but a simple musician, who had made essays in criticisms and tried to make a composer out of Siegfried Wagner)

to provide with incidental music. Mr. Humperdinck took his task seriously. The play, with some
incidental music, was two years old before Mr.
Humperdinck had his overture ready. He had tried
a new experiment, which proved a failure. The
second and third acts had their preludes, and the
songs of the minstrel had their melodies and accom-
paniments, and all the principal scenes had been
provided with illustrative music in the Wagnerian
manner, with this difference, that the dialogue had
been "pointed," as a church musician would say —
that is, the rhythm was indicated with exactness,
and even the variations of pitch, though it was understood that the purpose was not to achieve song, but
an intensified utterance, halfway between speech
and song. This was melodrama, as Herr Humperdinck conceived it and as it had no doubt existed
for ages — ever since the primitive Greek drama, in
fact. It is easy to understand how Herr Humperdinck came to believe in the possibility of an art-
form which, though accepted, for temporary effect,
by Beethoven and Cherubini, and used for ballads
with greater or less success by Schumann, had been
harshly rejected by his great model and master,
Wagner. Humperdinck lives in Germany, where
in nearly every theatre there is more or less of an
amalgamation of the spoken drama and the opera —
where choristers play small parts and actors, though
not professional singers, sing when not too much is
required of them. And yet Herr Humperdinck

found out that he had asked too much of his actors
with his "pointed" and at times intoned declamation, and "Königskinder" did not have to come to
America to learn that the compromise was a failure.
No doubt Herr Humperdinck thought of turning so
beautiful a play into an opera then, but it seems to
have required the stimulus which finally came from
New York to persuade him to carry out the operatic
idea, which is more than suggested in the score as
it lies before me in its original shape, into a thorough
lyric drama.   The set pieces which had lived in the
interim in the concert-room were transferred into
the opera-score with trifling alterations and condensations and so were the set songs.   As for the
rest it needed only that note-heads be supplied to
some of the portions of the dialogue which Humperdinck had designed for melodic declamation to have
those portions ready for the opera.   Here an example : —

Willst du mein Mai-en-buh-le sein,   du Blu-men-wei-che?

A German opera can generally stand severer criticism than one in another language, because there is
a more strict application of principles in Germany
when it comes to writing a lyric drama than in any
other country.   So in the present instance there is no
need to conceal the fact that there are outbreaks of
eroticism and offences against the German language

which are none the less flagrant and censurable because they are, to some extent, concealed under the thin veneer of the allegory and symbolism which every reader must have recognized as running through the play. This is, in a manner, Wagnerian, as so much of the music is Wagnerian — especially that of the second act, which because it calls up scenes from the "Meistersinger" must also necessarily call up music from the same comedy. But there is little cause here for quarrel with Professor Humperdinck. He has applied the poetical principle of Wagner to the fairy tale which is so closely related to the myth, and he has with equal consistency applied Wagner's constructive methods musically and dramatically. It is to his great honor that, of all of Wagner's successors, he has been the only one to do so successfully.

The story of "Königskinder," though it belongs to the class of fairy tales of which "Hänsel und Gretel" is so striking and beautiful an example, is not to be found as the author presents it in the literature of German *Märchen*. Mme. Bernstein has drawn its elements from many sources and blended them with the utmost freedom. To avoid a misunderstanding Germans will insist that the title be used without the article, for "Die Königskinder" or "Zwei Königskinder" both suggest the simple German form of the old tale of Hero and Leander, with which story, of course, it has nothing whatever to do. But if literary criticism forbids association between Humperdinck's two operas, musical criticism compels it. Many of the characters in the operas are close relations, dramatically as well as musically — the royal children themselves, the witches, of course, and the broom-makers. The rest of the characters have been taken from Wagner's "Meistersinger" picture book; the citizens of Hellabrunn are Nuremberg's burghers, the city's councillors, the old master singers. The musical idiom is Humperdinck's, though its method of employment is Wagner's. But here lies its charm: Though the composer hews to a theoretical line, he does it freely, naturally, easily, and always with the principle of musical beauty as well as that of dramatic truthfulness and propriety in view. His people's voices float on a symphonic stream, but the voices of the instruments, while they sing on in endless melody, use the idiom which nature gave them. There is admirable characterization in the orchestral music, but it is music for all that; it never descends to mere noise, designed to keep up an irritation of the nerves.

CHAPTER XV

FROM whatever point of view it may be considered Mossourgsky's opera "Boris Godounoff" is an extraordinary work. It was brought to the notice of the people of the United States by a first performance at the Metropolitan Opera House, in New York, on March 19, 1913, but intelligence concerning its character had come to observers of musical doings abroad by reports touching performances in Paris and London. It is possible, even likely, that at all the performances of the work outside of Russia those who listened to it with the least amount of intellectual sophistication derived the greatest pleasure from it, though to them its artistic deficiencies must also have been most obvious. Against these deficiencies, however, it presented itself, first of all, as a historical play shot through and through with a large theme, which, since it belongs to tragedy, is universal and unhampered by time or place or people. To them it had something of the sweep, dignity, and solemnity and also something of the dramatic incongruity and lack of cohesion of a Shakespearian drama as contradistinguished from the coherence of purpose and manner of a modern drama.

To them also it had much strangeness of style, a style which was not easily reconciled to anything with which the modern stage had made them familiar. They saw and heard the chorus enter into the action, not for the purpose of spectacular pageantry, nor as hymners of the achievements of the principal actors in the story, but as participants. They heard unwonted accents from these actors and saw them behave in conduct which from moment to moment appeared strangely contradictory. There were mutterings of popular discontent, which, under threats, gave way to jubilant acclamation in the first great scenes in the beginning of the opera. There were alternate mockeries and adulations in the next scene in which the people figured; and running through other scenes from invisible singers came ecclesiastical chants, against which were projected, not operatic song in the old conception, but long passages of heightened speech, half declamatory, half musical. A multitude cringed before upraised knouts and fell on its knees before the approach of a man whose agents swung the knotted cords; anon they acclaimed the man who sought to usurp a throne and overwhelmed with ridicule a village imbecile, who was yet supposed because of his mental weakness to be possessed of miraculous prescience, and therefore to have a prevision of what was to follow the usurpation. They saw the incidents of the drama moving past their eyes within a framework of barbaric splendor typical of a wonderful political past, an amazing political present, and possibly prophetic of a still more amazing political future.

These happily ingenuous spectators saw an historical personage racked by conscience, nerve-torn by spectres, obsessed by superstitions, strong in position achieved, yet pathetically sweet and moving in his exhibition of paternal love, and going to destruction through remorse for crime committed. They were troubled by no curious questionings as to the accuracy of the historical representation. The *Boris Godounoff* before them was a remorse-stricken regicide, whose good works, if he did any, had to be summed up for their imagination in the fact that he loved his son. In all this, and also in some of its music, the new opera was of the opera operatic. But to the unhappily disingenuous (or perhaps it would be better to say, to the instructed) there was much more in the new opera; and it was this more which so often gave judgment pause, even while it stimulated interest and irritated curiosity. It was a pity that a recent extraordinary outburst of enthusiasm about a composer and an opera should have had the effect of distorting their vision and disturbing their judgment.

There was a reason to be suspicious touching this enthusiasm, because of its origin. It came from France and not from the home land of the author of the play or the composer of the music. Moreover, it was largely based upon an element which has as little genuineness in France as a basis of judgment (and which must therefore be set down largely as an affectation) as in America. Loud hallelujahs have been raised in praise of Moussorgsky because, discarding conventional law, he vitalized the music of the lyric poem and also the dramatic line, by making it the emotional flowering of the spoken word. When it became necessary for the precious inner brotherhood of Frenchmen who hold burning incense sticks under each others' noses to acclaim "Pelléas et Mélisande" as a new and beautiful thing in dramatic music, it was announced that Moussorgsky was like Debussy in that he had demonstrated in his songs and his operas that vocal melody should and could be written in accordance with the rhythm and accents of the words. We had supposed that we had learned that lesson not only from Gluck and Wagner, but from every true musical dramatist that ever lived! And when the Frenchmen (and their feeble echoers in England and America) began to cry out that the world make obeisance to Moussorgsky on that score, there was no wonder that those whose eagerness to enjoy led them to absorb too much information should ask how this marvellous psychical assonance between word and tone was to be conveyed to their unfortunate sense and feeling after the original Russian word had been transmogrified into French or English. In New York the opera, which we know to be saturated in some respects with Muscovitism, or Slavicism, and which we have every reason to believe is also so saturated in its musico-verbal essence, was sung in Italian. With the change some of the character that ought to make it dear to the Russian heart must have evaporated. It is even likely that vigorous English would have been a better vehicle than the "soft, bastard Latin" for the forceful utterances of the operatic people.

It is a pity that a suspicion of disingenuousness and affectation should force itself upon one's thoughts in connection with the French enthusiasm over Moussorgsky; but it cannot be avoided. So far as Moussorgsky reflects anything in his art, it is realism or naturalism, and the latter element is not dominant in French music now, and is not likely to be so long as the present tendency toward sublimated subjectivism prevails. Debussy acclaimed Moussorgsky enthusiastically a dozen years ago, but for all that Moussorgsky and Debussy are antipodes in art — they represent extremes.

It is much more likely that outside of its purely literary aspect (a large aspect in every respect in France) the Moussorgsky cult of the last few years was a mere outgrowth of the political affiliation between France and Russia; as such it may be looked upon in the same light as the sudden appreciation of Berlioz which was a product of the Chauvinism which followed the Franco-Prussian War. It is easy even for young people of the day in which I write to remember when a Wagner opera at the Académie Nationale raised a riot, and when the dances at the Moulin Rouge and such places could not begin until the band had played the Russian national hymn.

Were it not for considerations of this sort it would be surprising to contemplate the fact that Moussorgsky has been more written and talked about in France than he was in his native Russia, and that even his friend Rimsky-Korsakoff, to whose revision of the score "Boris Godounoff" owes its continued existence, has been subjected to much rude criticism because of his work, though we can only think of it as taken up in a spirit of affection and admiration. He and the Russians, with scarcely an exception, say that his labors were in the line of purification and rectification; but the modern extremists will have it that by remedying its crudities of harmonization and instrumentation he weakened it — that what he thought its artistic blemishes were its virtues. Of that we are in no position to speak, nor ought any one be rash enough to make the proclamation until the original score is published, and then only a Russian or a musician familiar with the Russian tongue and its genius.   The production of the opera outside of Russia and in a foreign language ought to furnish an occasion to demand a stay of the artistic cant which is all too common just now in every country.

We are told that "Boris Godounoff" is the first real Russian opera that America has ever heard. In a sense that may be true.   The present generation has heard little operatic music by Russian composers. Rubinstein's "Nero" was not Russian music in any respect. "Pique Dame," by Tschaikowsky, also performed at the Metropolitan Opera House, had little in it that could be recognized as characteristically Russian. "Eugene Onegin" we know only from concert performances, and its Muscovitism was a negligible quantity. The excerpts from other Russian operas have been few and they demonstrated nothing, though in an intermezzo from Tschaikowsky's "Mazeppa," descriptive of the battle of Poltava, which has been heard here, we met with the strong choral tune which gives great animation to the most stirring scene in "Boris" — the acclamation of the Czar by the populace in the first act. Of this something more presently. There were American representations, however, of a Russian opera which in its day was more popular than "Boris" has ever been; but that was so long ago that all memories of it have died, and even the records are difficult to reach. Some fifty years ago a Russian company came to these shores and performed Verstoffsky's "Askold's Tomb," an opera which was republished as late as 1897 and which within the first twenty-five years of its existence had 400 performances in Moscow and 200 in St. Petersburg. Some venturesome critics have hailed Verstoffsky as even more distinctively a predecessor of Moussorgsky than Glinka; but the clamor of those who are preaching loudly that art must not exist for art's sake, and that the ugly is justified by the beauty of ugliness, has silenced the voices of these critical historians.

This may thus far have seemed a long and discursive disquisition on the significance of the new opera; but the questions to which the production of "Boris Godounoff" give rise are many and grave, especially in the present state of our operatic activities. They have a strong bearing on the problem of nationalism in opera, of which those in charge of our operatic affairs appear to take a careless view. Aside from all æsthetic questions, "Boris Godounoff" bears heavily on that problem. It is a work crude and fragmentary in structure, but it is tremendously puissant in its preachment of nationalism; and it is strong there not so much because of its story and the splendid barbarism of its external integument as because of its nationalism, which is proclaimed in the use of Russian folk-song. All previous experiments in this line become insignificant in comparison with it, and it is questionable if any other body of folk-song offers such an opportunity to the operatic composer as does the Russian. The hero of the opera is in dramatic stature (or at least in emotional content) a *Macbeth* or a *Richard III;* his utterances are frequently poignant and heart searching in the extreme; his dramatic portrayal by M. Chaliapine in Europe and Mr. Didur in America is so gripping as to call up memories of some of the great English tragedians of the past. But we cannot speak of the psychology of the musical setting of his words because we have been warned that it roots deeply in the accents and inflections of a language with which we are un-

familiar and which was not used in the performance.
But the music of the choral masses, the songs sung
in the intimacy of the *Czar Boris's* household, the
chants of the monks, needed not to be strange to
any student of folk-song, nor could their puissance
be lost upon the musically unlettered. In the old
Kolyáda Song "Sláva" [1] with which *Boris* is greeted
by the populace, as well as in the wild shoutings of
the Polish vagrom men and women in the scene
before the last, it is impossible not to hear an out-
pouring of that spirit of which Tolstoi wrote: "In
it is yearning without end, without hope; also
power invincible, the fateful stamp of destiny, iron
preordination, one of the fundamental principles of
our nationality with which it is possible to explain
much that in Russian life seems incomprehensible."

No other people have such a treasure of folk-song
to draw on as that thus characterized, and it is
not likely that any other people will develop a
national school of opera on the lines which lie open
to the Russian composer, and which the Russian
composer has been encouraged to exploit by his
government for the last twenty years or more.

It is possible that some critics, actuated by political
rather than artistic considerations, will find reasons

[1] Lovers of chamber music know this melody from its use in
the allegretto in Beethoven's E minor Quartet dedicated to
Count Rasoumowski, where it appears thus:—

for the present condition of Moussorgsky's score in the attitude of the Russian government. It is said that court intrigues had much to do with the many changes which the score had to undergo before it became entirely acceptable to the powers that be in the Czar's empire. Possibly. But every change which has come under the notice of this reviewer has been to its betterment and made for its practical presentation. It is said that the popular scenes were curtailed because they represented the voice of the democracy. But there is still so much choral work in the opera that the judgment of the operatic audiences of to-day is likely to pronounce against it measurably on that account. For, splendid as the choral element in the work is, a chorus is not looked upon with admiration as a dramatic element by the ordinary opera lover. There was a lack of the feminine element in the opera, and to remedy this Moussorgsky had to introduce the Polish bride of the *False Dmitri* and give the pair a love scene, and incidentally a polonaise; but the love scene is uninteresting until its concluding measures, and these are too Meyerbeerian to call for comment beyond the fact that Meyerbeer, the much contemned, would have done better. As for the polonaise, Tschaikowsky has written a more brilliant one for his "Eugene Onegin."

The various scores of the opera which have been printed show that Moussorgsky, with all his genius, was at sea even when it came to applying the prin-

ciples of the Young Russian School, of which he is set
down as a strong prop, to dramatic composition.
With all his additions, emendations, and rearrange-
ments, his opera still falls much short of being a
dramatic unit. It is a more loosely connected series
of scenes, from the drama of Boris Godounoff and
the false Dmitri, than Boito's "Mefistofele" is of
Goethe's "Faust." Had he had his own way the
opera would have ended with the scene in which
Dmitri proceeds to Moscow amid the huzzas of a
horde of Polish vagabonds, and we should have had
neither a *Boris* nor a *Dmitri* opera, despite the
splendid opportunities offered by both characters.
It was made a *Boris* opera by bringing it to an end
with the death of *Boris* and leaving everything
except the scenes in which the *Czar* declines the imperial crown, then accepts it, and finally dies of a
tortured conscience, to serve simply as intermezzi,
in which for the moment the tide of tragedy is turned
aside. This and the glimpse into the paternal
heart of the *Czar* is the only and beautiful purpose of
the domestic scene, in which the lighter and more
cheerful element of Russian folk-song is introduced.

At the first American performance of "Boris
Godounoff" the cast was as follows: —

Boris................................Adamo Didur
Theodore..............................Anna Case
Xenia...........................Lenora Sparkes
The Nurse.........................Maria Duchêne
Marina..............................Louise Homer

Schouisky...............................Angelo Bada
Tchelkaloff......................Vincenzo Reschiglian
Pimenn................................Léon Rothier
Dmitri.....................Paul Althouse (his debut)
Varlaam........................Andrea de Segurola
Missail...............................Pietro Audisio
The Innkeeper......................Jeanne Maubourg
The Simpleton.........................Albert Reiss
A Police Officer..........................Giulio Rossi
A Court Officer.................... Leopoldo Mariani
Lovitzky...... ⎫   ⎧ V. Reschiglian
Tcerniakowsky ⎭Two Jesuits.......... ⎩ Louis Kreidler

Conductor : Arturo Toscanini

CHAPTER XVI

"MADAME SANS-GÊNE" AND OTHER OPERAS BY GIORDANO

THE opera-goers of New York enjoyed a novel experience when Giordano's "Madame Sans-Gêne" had its first performance on any stage in their presence at the Metropolitan Opera House on January 25, 1915. It was the first time that a royal and imperial personage who may be said to live freshly and vividly in the minds of the people of this generation as well as in their imaginations appeared before them to sing his thoughts and feelings in operatic fashion. At first blush it seemed as if a singing Bonaparte was better calculated to stir their risibilities than their interest or sympathies; and this may, indeed, have been the case; but at any rate they had an opportunity to make the acquaintance of Napoleon before he rose to imperial estate. But, in all seriousness, it is easier to imagine the figure which William II of Germany would cut on the operatic stage than the "grand, gloomy, and peculiar" Corsican. The royal people with whom the operatic public is familiar as a rule are sufficiently surrounded by the mists of antiquity and obscurity that the

221

contemplation of them arouse little thought of the incongruity which their appearance as operatic heroes ought to create. *Henry the Fowler* in "Lohengrin," *Mark* in "Tristan und Isolde," the unnumbered *Pharaoh* in "Aïda," *Herod* in "Salomé" and "Hérodiade," and the few other kings, if there are any more with whom the present generation of opera-goers have a personal acquaintance, so to speak, are more or less merely poetical creations whom we seldom if ever think of in connection with veritable history. Even *Boris Godounoff* is to us more a picture out of a book, like the *Macbeth* whom he so strongly resembles from a theatrical point of view, than the monarch who had a large part in the making of the Russian people. The Roman censorship prevented us long ago from making the acquaintance of the Gustavus of Sweden whom Ankerström stabbed to death at a masked ball, by transmogrifying him into the absurdly impossible figure of a *Governor of Boston;* and the *Claudius* of Ambroise Thomas's opera is as much a ghost as *Hamlet's* father, while Debussy's blind *King* is as much an abstraction as is *Mélisande* herself.

Operatic dukes we know in plenty, though most of them have come out of the pages of romance and are more or less acceptable according to the vocal ability of their representatives. When Caruso sings "La donna è mobile" we care little for the profligacy of Verdi's *Duke of Mantua* and do not inquire whether or not such an individual ever lived. Moussorgsky's

Czar Boris ought to interest us more, however. The great bell-tower in the Kremlin which he built, and the great bell — a shattered monument of one of his futile ambitions — have been seen by thousands of travellers who never took the trouble to learn that the tyrant who had the bell cast laid a serfdom upon the Russian people which endured down to our day. Boris, by the way, picturesque and dramatic figure that he is as presented to us in history, never got upon the operatic stage until Moussorgsky took him in hand. Two hundred years ago a great German musician, Mattheson, as much scholar as composer if not more, set him to music, but the opera was never performed. Peter the Great, who came a century after Boris, lived a life more calculated to invite the attention of opera writers, but even he escaped the clutches of dramatic composers except Lortzing, who took advantage of the romantic episode of Peter's service as ship carpenter in Holland to make him the hero of one of the most sparkling of German comic operas. Lortzing had a successor in the Irishman T. S. Cooke, but his opera found its way into the limbo of forgotten things more than a generation ago, while Lortzing's still lives on the stage of Germany. Peter deserved to be celebrated in music, for it was in his reign that polyphonic music, albeit of the Italian order, was introduced into the Russian church and modern instrumental music effected an entrance into his empire. But I doubt if Peter was sincerely musical; in his youth he heard

only music of the rudest kind. He was partial to
the bagpipes and, like Nero, played upon that
instrument.

To come back to Bonaparte and music. "Madame Sans-Gêne" is an operatic version of the drama
which Sardou developed out of a little one-act play
dealing with a partly fictitious, partly historical story
in which Napoleon, his marshal Lefèbvre, and a laun-
dress were the principal figures. Whether or not
the great Corsican could be justified as a character
in a lyric drama was a mooted question when Giordano conceived the idea of making an opera out of
the play. It is said that Verdi remarked something
to the effect that the question depended upon what
he would be called upon to sing, and how he would be
expected to sing it. The problem was really not a
very large or difficult one, for all great people are
turned into marionettes when transformed into
operatic heroes.

In the palmy days of *bel canto* no one would have
raised the question at all, for then the greatest characters in history moved about the stage in stately
robes and sang conventional arias in the conventional
manner. The change from old-fashioned opera to
regenerated lyric drama might have simplified the
problem for Giordano, even if his librettist had not
already done so by reducing Napoleon to his lowest
terms from a dramatic as well as historical point of
view. The heroes of eighteenth-century opera were
generally feeble-minded lovers and nothing more;

Giordano's Napoleon is only a jealous husband who helps out in the dénouement of a play which is concerned chiefly with other people.

In turning Sardou's dramatic personages into operatic puppets a great deal of bloodletting was necessary and a great deal of the characteristic charm of the comedy was lost, especially in the cases of *Madame Sans-Gêne* herself and *Napoleon's* sister; but enough was left to make a practicable opera. There were the pictures of all the plebeians who became great folk later concerned in the historical incidents which lifted them up. There were also the contrasted pictures which resulted from the great transformation, and it was also the ingratiating incident of the devotion of *Lefèbvre* to the stout-hearted, honest little woman of the people who had to try to be a duchess. All this was fair operatic material, though music has a strange capacity for refining stage characters as well as for making them colorless. Giordano could not do himself justice as a composer without refining the expression of *Caterina Huebscher,* and so his *Duchess of Dantzic* talks a musical language at least which Sardou's washerwoman could not talk and remain within the dramatic verities. Therefore we have "Madame Sans-Gêne" with a difference, but not one that gave any more offence than operatic treatment of other fine plays have accustomed us to.

To dispose of the artistic merits of the opera as briefly as possible, it may be said that in more ways

Q

than one Giordano has in this work harked back to
"Andrea Chenier," the first of his operas which had
a hearing in America.   The parallel extends to some
of the political elements of the book as well as its
musical investiture with its echoes of the popular airs
of the period of the French Revolution.   The style
of writing is also there, though applied, possibly,
with more mature and refined skill.   I cannot say
with as much ingenuousness and freshness of invention, however.   Its spirit in the first act, and largely
in the second, is that of the *opéra bouffe*, but there
are many pages of "Madame Sans-Gêne" which I
would gladly exchange for any one of the melodies of
Lecocq, let us say in "La Fille de Mme. Angot."
Like all good French music which uses and imitates
them, it is full of crisp rhythms largely developed from
the old dances which, originally innocent, were degraded to base uses by the *sans-culottes;* and so there
is an abundance of life and energy in the score though
little of the distinction, elegance, and grace that have
always been characteristic of French music, whether
high-born or low.   The best melody in the modern
Italian vein flows in the second act when the genuine
affection and fidelity of *Caterina* find expression
and where a light touch is combined with considerable warmth of feeling and a delightful daintiness of
orchestral color.   Much of this is out of harmony with
the fundamental character of Sardou's woman, but
music cannot deny its nature.   Only a Moussorgsky
could make a drunken monk talk truthfully in music.

If Giordano's opera failed to make a profound impression on the New York public, it was not because that public had not had opportunity to learn the quality of his music. His "Andrea Chenier" had been produced at the Academy of Music as long before as November 13, 1896. With it the redoubtable Colonel Mapleson went down to his destruction in America. It was one of the many strange incidents in the career of Mr. Oscar Hammerstein as I have related them in my book entitled "Chapters of Opera"[1] that it should have been brought back by him twelve years later for a single performance at the Manhattan Opera House. In the season of 1916–1917 it was incorporated in the repertory of the Boston-National Opera Company and carried to the principal cities of the country. On December 16, 1906, Mr. Heinrich Conried thought that the peculiar charms of Madame Cavalieri, combined with the popularity of Signor Caruso, might give habitation to Giordano's setting of an opera book made out of Sardou's "Fédora"; but it endured for only four performances in the season of 1906–1907 and three in the next, in which Conried's career came to an end. In reviving "Andrea Chenier" Mr. Hammerstein may have had visions of future triumphs for its composer, for a few weeks before (on February 5, 1908) he had brought forward the same composer's "Siberia," which gave some promise of life, though it died with the season that saw its birth.

[1] New York, Henry Holt & Co.

The critical mind seems disposed to look with kindness upon new works in proportion as they fall back in the corridors of memory; and so I am inclined to think that of the four operas by Giordano which I have heard "Andrea Chenier" gives greatest promise of a long life. The attempt to put music to "Fédora" seemed to me utterly futile. Only those moments were musical in the accepted sense of the word when the action of the drama ceased, as in the case of the intermezzo, or when the old principles of operatic construction waked into life again as in the confession of the hero-lover. Here, moreover, there comes into the score an element of novelty, for the confession is extorted from *Lorris* while a virtuoso is entertaining a drawing-roomful of people with a set pianoforte solo. As for the rest of the opera, it seems sadly deficient in melody beautiful either in itself or as an expression of passion. "Andrea Chenier" has more to commend it. To start with, there is a good play back of it, though the verities of history were not permitted to hamper the imagination of Signor Illica, the author of the book. The hero of the opera is the patriotic poet who fell under the guillotine in 1794 at the age of thirty-two. The place which Saint-Beuve gave him in French letters is that of the greatest writer of classic verse after Racine and Boileau. The operatic story is all fiction, more so, indeed, than that of "Madame Sans-Gêne." As a matter of fact, the veritable Chenier was thrown into prison on the accusation of having sheltered a political criminal, and was beheaded together with twenty-three others on a charge of having engaged in a conspiracy while in prison. In the opera he does not die for political reasons, though they are alleged as a pretext, but because he has crossed the love-path of a leader of the revolution.

When Giordano composed "Siberia," he followed the example of Mascagni and Puccini (if he did not set the example for them) by seeking local color and melodic material in the folk-songs of the country in which his scene was laid. Puccini went to Japan for musical ideas and devices to trick out his "Madama Butterfly" as Mascagni had done in "Iris." Giordano, illustrating a story of political oppression in "Siberia," called in the aid of Russian melodies. His exiles sing the heavy-hearted measures of the bargemen of the Volga, "Ay ouchnem," the forceful charm of which few Russian composers have been able to resist. He introduced also strains of Easter music from the Greek church, the popular song known among the Germans as "Schöne Minka" and the "Glory" song (*Slava*) which Moussorgsky had forged into a choral thunderbolt in his "Boris Godounoff." It is a stranger coincidence that the "Slava" melody should have cropped up in the operas of Giordano and Moussorgsky than that the same revolutionary airs should pepper the pages of "Madame Sans-Gêne" and "Andrea Chenier." These operas are allied in subject and period and the same style of composition is followed in both.

Chenier goes to his death in the opera to the tune of the "Marseillaise" and the men march past the windows of *Caterina Huebscher's* laundry singing the refrain of Roget de Lisle's hymn. But Giordano does not make extensive use of the tune in "Madame Sans-Gêne." It appears literally at the place mentioned and surges up with fine effect in a speech in which the *Duchess of Dantzic* overwhelms the proud sisters of Napoleon; but that is practically all. The case is different with two other revolutionary airs. The first crash of the orchestra launches us into "La Carmagnole," whose melody provides the thematic orchestral substratum for nearly the entire first scene. It is an innocent enough tune, differing little from hundreds of French vaudeville melodies of its period, but Giordano injects vitriol into its veins by his harmonies and orchestration. With all its innocence this was the tune which came from the raucous throats of politically crazed men and women while noble heads tumbled into the bloody sawdust, while the spoils of the churches were carried into the National Convention in 1793, and to which "several members, quitting their curule chairs, took the hands of girls flaunting in priests' vestures" and danced a wild rout, as did other mad wretches when a dancer was worshipped as the Goddess of Reason in the Cathedral of Notre Dame.

Caterina's account of the rude familiarity with which she is treated by the soldiery (I must assume a knowledge of Sardou's play which the opera follows) is set to a melody of a Russian folk-song cast in the treatment of which Russian influences may also be felt; but with the first shouts of the mob attacking the Tuileries in the distance the characteristic rhythmical *motif* of the "Ça ira" is heard muttering in the basses. Again a harmless tune which in its time was perverted to a horrible use; a lively little contradance which graced many a cotillion in its early days, but which was roared and howled by the mob as it carried the beauteous head of the Lamballe through the streets of Paris on a pike and thrust it almost into the face of Marie Antoinette.

Of such material and a pretty little dance ("La Fricassée") is the music of the first act, punctuated by cannon shots, made. It is all rhythmically stirring, it flows spiritedly, energetically along with the current of the play, never retarding it for a moment, but, unhappily, never sweetening it with a grain of pretty sentiment or adorning it with a really graceful contour. There is some graciousness in the court scene, some archness and humor in the scene in which the *Duchess of Dantzic* submits to the adornment of her person, some dramatically strong declamation in the speeches of *Napoleon*, some simulation of passion in the love passages of *Lefèbvre* and of *Neipperg;* but as a rule the melodic flood never reaches high tide.

CHAPTER XVII

TWO OPERAS BY WOLF-FERRARI

WHEN the operas of Ermanno Wolf-Ferrari came to America (his beautiful setting of the "Vita Nuova" was already quite widely known at the time), it was thought singular and somewhat significant that though the operas had all been composed to Italian texts they should have their first Italian performances in this country. This was the case with "Le Donne Curiose," heard at the Metropolitan Opera House, New York, on January 3, 1912; of "Il Segreto di Susanna," which the Chicago-Philadelphia Opera Company brought to New York after giving it a hearing in its home cities, in February, 1912; of "I Giojelli della Madonna" first produced in Berlin in December, 1911, and in Chicago a few weeks later. A fourth opera, "L'Amore Medico," had its first representation at the Metropolitan Opera House, New York, on March 25, 1914.

The circumstance to which I have alluded as worthy of comment was due, I fancy, more to the business methods of modern publishers than to a want of appreciation of the operas in Italy, though

A PAGE OF THE SCORE OF THE GERMAN "DONNE CURIOSE"

Signor Wolf-Ferrari sought to meet the taste of his countrymen (assuming that the son of a German father and a Venetian mother is to be set down as an Italian) when he betrayed the true bent of his genius and sought to join the ranks of the Italian veritists in his "Giojelli della Madonna." However, that is not the question I am desirous to discuss just now when the first impressions of "Le Donne Curiose" come flocking back to my memory. The book is a paraphrase of Goldoni's comedy of the same name, made (and very deftly made) for the composer by Count Luigi Sugana. It turns on the curiosity of a group of women concerning the doings of their husbands and sweethearts at a club from which they are excluded. The action is merely a series of incidents in which the women (the wives by rifling the pockets of their husbands, the maidens by wheedling, cajoling, and playing upon the feelings of their sweethearts) obtain the keys of the club-room, and effect an entrance only to find that instead of gambling, harboring mistresses, seeking the philosopher's stone, or digging for treasure, as is variously suspected, the men are enjoying an innocent supper. In their eagerness to see all that is going on, the women betray their presence. Then there follow scoldings, contrition, forgiveness, a graceful minuet, and the merriment runs out in a wild furlana.

Book and score of the opera hark back a century or more in their methods of expression. The in-

cidents of the old comedy are as loosely strung
together as those of "Le Nozze di Figaro," and the
parallel is carried further by the similarity between
the instrumental apparatus of Mozart and Wolf-
Ferrari and the dependence of both on melody,
rather than orchestral or harmonic device, as the
life-blood of the music upon which the comedy
floats. It is Mozart's orchestra that the modern
composer uses ("the only proper orchestra for
comedy," as Berlioz said), eschewing even those
"epical instruments," the trombones. It would not
do to push the parallel too far, though a keen listener
might feel tempted also to see a point of semblance
in the Teutonism which tinctures the Italian music
of both men; a Teutonism which adds an ingredient
more to the taste of other peoples than that of the
people whose language is employed. But while the
Italianism of Mozart was wholly the product of
the art-spirit of his time, the Teutonism of Wolf-
Ferrari is a heritage from his German father and
its Italianism partakes somewhat of the nature of a
reversion to old ideals from which even his mother's
countrymen have departed. There is an almost
amusing illustration of this in the paraphrase of
Goldoni's comedy which the composer took as a
libretto. The *Leporello* of Da Ponte and Mozart
has his prototype in the *Arlecchino* of the classic
Italian comedy, but he has had to submit to so
great a metamorphosis as to make him scarcely
recognizable. But in the modern "Donne Curiose"

we have not only the old figure down to his conventional dress and antics, but also his companions *Pantaloon* and *Columbine*. All this, however, may be better enjoyed by those who observe them in the representation than those who will only read about them, no matter how deftly the analysis may be made.

It is Mozart's media and Mozart's style which Wolf-Ferrari adopts, but there are traces also of the idioms of others who have been universal musicians rather than specifically Italian. Like Nicolai's "O süsse Anna!" (Shakespeare's "Oh, Sweet Anne Page"), Wolf-Ferrari's *Florindo* breathes out his languishing "Ah, Rosaura!" And in the lively chatter of the women there is frequently more than a suggestion of the lively gossip of Verdi's merry wives in his incomparable "Falstaff." Wolf-Ferrari is neither a Mozart nor a Verdi, not even a Nicolai, as a melodist, but he is worthy of being bracketed with them, because as frankly as they he has spoken the musical language which to him seemed a proper investiture of his comedy, and like them has made that language characteristic of the comedy's personages and illustrative of its incidents. He has been brave enough not to fear being called a reactionary, knowing that there is always progress in the successful pursuit of beauty.

The advocates of opera sung in the language native to the hearers may find an eloquent argument in "Le Donne Curiose," much of whose humor lies in the text and is lost to those who cannot under-

stand it despite the obviousness of its farcical action.
On the other hand, a feeling of gratitude must have
been felt by many others that they were not compelled to hear the awkward commonplaces of the
English translation of the libretto. The German
version, in which the opera had its first hearing in
Munich six years before, is in a vastly different
case — neither uncouth nor halting, even though it
lacks the characteristic fluency essential to Italian
opera buffa; yet no more than did the speech of
most of the singers at the Metropolitan performance.
The ripple and rattle of the Italian *parlando* seem
to be possible only to Italian tongues.

The Mozartian type of music is illustrated not
only in the character of many of its melodies, but
also in the use of *motivi* in what may be called the
dramatic portions — the fleet flood upon which the
dialogue dances with a light buoyancy that is delightfully refreshing. These *motivi* are not used in
the Wagnerian manner, but as every change of
situation or emotion is characterized in Mozart's
marvellous ensembles by the introduction of a
new musical idea, so they are in his modern disciple's.
All of them are finely characteristic, none more so
than the comical cackle so often heard from the
oboe in the scenes wherein the women gossip about
the imaginary doings of the men — an intentional
echo, it would almost seem, of the theme out of
which Rameau made his dainty harpsichord piece
known as "La Poule." The motto of the club,

"Bandie xe le done," is frequently proclaimed with more or less pomposity; *Florindo's* "Ah, Rosaura," with its dramatic descent, lends sentimental feeling to the love music, and the sprightly rhythm which accompanies the pranks of *Colombina* keeps much of the music bubbling with merriment. In the beginning of the third act, not only the instrumental introduction, but much of the delightful music which follows, is permeated with atmosphere and local color derived from a familiar Venetian barcarolle ("La biondina in gondoleta"), but the musical loveliness reaches its climax in the sentimental scenes — a quartet, a solo by *Rosaura*, and a duet, in which there breathes the sympathetic spirit of Smetana as well as Mozart.[1]

[1] The cast at the first performance at the Metropolitan Opera House was as follows: —

Ottavio	Adamo Dídur
Beatrice	Jeanne Maubourg
Rosaura	Geraldine Farrar
Florindo	Hermann Jadlowker
Pantalone	Antonio Pini-Corso
Lelio	Antonio Scotti
Leandro	Angelo Bada
Colombina	Bella Alten
Eleonora	Rita Fornia
Arlecchino	Andrea de Segurola
Asdrubale	Pietro Audisio
Almoro	Lambert Murphy
Alvise	Charles Hargreaves
Lunardo	Vincenzo Reschiglian
Momolo	Paolo Ananian
Menego	Giulio Rossi
Un Servitore	Stefen Buckreus

Conductor — Arturo Toscanini.

In "Le Donne Curiose," the gondoliers sing their barcarolle and compel even the cynic of the drama to break out into an enthusiastic exclamation: "Oh, beautiful Venice!" The world has heard more of the natural beauties of Naples than of the artificial ones of Venice, but when Naples is made the scene of a drama of any kind it seems that its attractions for librettist and composer lie in the vulgarity and vice, libertinism and lust, the wickedness and wantonness, of a portion of its people rather than in the loveliness of character which such a place might or ought to inspire.

Perhaps it was not altogether surprising that when Wolf-Ferrari turned from Venice and "Le Donne Curiose" to "I Giojelli della Madonna" with Naples as a theatre for his drama he should not only change the style of his music, but also revert to the kind of tale which his predecessors in the field seem to have thought appropriate to the place which we have been told all of us should see once and die out of sheer ecstasy over its beauty. But why are only the slums of Naples deemed appropriate for dramatic treatment?

How many stories of Neapolitan life have been told in operas since Auber wrote his "La Muette di Portici" I do not know; doubtless many whose existence ended with the *stagione* for which they were composed. But it is a singular fact bearing on the present discussion that when the young "veritists" of Italy broke loose after the success of

Mascagni's "Cavalleria rusticana" there came almost a universal desire to rush to the Neapolitan shambles for subjects. New York has been spared all of these operas which I have described in an earlier chapter of this book, except the delectable "A Basso Porto" which Mr. Savage's company gave to us in English sixteen years ago; but never since.

Whether or not Wolf-Ferrari got the subject of "I Giojelli della Madonna" from the sources drawn on by his predecessors, I do not know. I believe that, like Leoncavallo, he has said that the story of his opera has a basis of fact. Be this as it may, it is certain that the composer called on two versifiers to help him out in making the book of the opera and that the story in its essence is not far removed from that of the French opera "Aphrodite," by Baron Erlanger. In that opera there is a rape of the adornments of a statue of Venus; in Wolf-Ferrari's work of the jewels enriching an effigy of the Virgin Mary. The story is not as filthy as the other plots rehearsed elsewhere, but in it there is the same striving after sharp ("piquant," some will say) contrasts, the blending of things sacred and profane, the mixture of ecclesiastical music and dances, and — what is most significant — the generous use of the style of melody which came in with Ponchielli and his pupils. In "I Giojelli della Madonna" a young woman discards the love of an honest-hearted man to throw herself,

out of sheer wantonness, into the arms of a blackguard dandy.   To win her heart through her love
of personal adornment the man of faithful mind
(the suggestion having come from his rival) does
the desperate deed of stealing for her the jewels of
the Madonna.   It is to be assumed that she re-
wards him for the sacrilegious act, but without
turning away from the blackguard, to whom she
grants a stolen interview during the time when
her true love is committing the crime.   But even
the vulgar and wicked companions of the dandy,
who is a leader among the Camorristi, turn from
her with horror when they discover the stolen
jewels around her neck, and she gives herself to
death in the sea.   Then the poor lover, placing the
jewels on the altar, invokes forgiveness, and, seeing
it in a ray of light which illumines them, thrusts a
dagger into his heart and dies at the feet of the
effigy of the goddess whom he had profaned.

The story would not take long in the telling
were it not tricked out with a multitude of incidents
designed to illustrate the popular life of Naples
during a festival.   Such things are old, familiar, and
unnecessary elements, in many cases not even
understood by the audience.   But with them Signor
Wolf-Ferrari manages to introduce most successfully
the atmosphere which he preserves even throughout
his tragical moments — the atmosphere of Neapolitan life and feeling.   The score is saturated with
Neapolitan folk-song.   I say Neapolitan rather than

R

Italian, because the mixed population of Naples
has introduced the elements which it would be rash
to define as always Italian, or even Latin. While
doing this the composer surrendered himself unreservedly and frankly to other influences. That
is one of the things which make him admirable in
the estimation of latter-day critics. In "Le Donne
Curiose" he is most lovingly frank in his compan-
ionship with Mozart. In "Il Segreto" there is a
combination of all the styles that prevailed from
Mozart to Donizetti. In "I Giojelli" no attempt
seems to have been made by him to avoid comparison with the composer who has made the most
successful attempt at giving musical expression to
a drama which fifty years ago the most farsighted
of critics would have set down as too rapid of movement to admit of adequate musical expression —
Mascagni and his "Cavalleria rusticana," of course.
But I am tempted to say that the most marvellous
faculty of Wolf-Ferrari is to do all these things
without sacrifice of his individuality. He has gone
further. In "La Vita Nuova" there is again an
entirely different man. Nothing in his operas
seems half so daring as everything in this cantata.
How he could produce a feeling of mediævalism in
the setting of Dante's sonnets and yet make use
of the most modern means of harmonization and
orchestration is still a mystery to this reviewer.
Yet, having done it long ago, he takes up the modern
style of Italian melody and blends it with the old

church song, so that while you are made to think one moment of Mascagni, you are set back a couple of centuries by the cadences and harmonies of the hymns which find their way into the merrymakings of the *festa*.   But everything appeals to the ear — nothing offends it, and for that, whatever our philosophical notions, we ought to be grateful to the melodiousness, the euphony, and the rich orchestration of the new opera.[1]

[1] The performances of "I Giojelli della Madonna" by the Chicago-Philadelphia Opera Company, as it was called in Chicago, the Philadelphia-Chicago Opera Company, as it was called in Philadelphia, were conducted by Cleofonte Campanini and the principal parts were in the hands of Carolina White, Louise Bèrat, Amadeo Bassi, and Mario Sammarco.

Mr. Krehbiel's other book, A Book of Operas, takes up the older classics such as *Faust*, *Aida* and the Wagnerian *Ring*.

Printed in the United States of America